Bubbles: The P

Bubbles: The Beggar's Lifeline

Tiger Man

Published by Tiger Man, 2024.

BUBBLES: THE BEGGAR'S LIFELINE

First edition. February 5, 2024.

ISBN: 979-8224952441

Written by Tiger Man.

This book is dedicated to my son David. No longer am I a ghost within such windswept corridors.

A special thanks to the rising of the Maureen sun, for its kind listening watch.

Chapter One

A Listening Watch

Well, here we are at last. Living in a world that we call home. Some would say we never have enough for our needs, except for Thomas-O, known to all in these parts as the Beggar of Blackthorn Hill. Such a life was seen as nothing more than shameful, disgusting, isolated. And so be it. As a perfect stranger once said, 'Are you not better off born lucky than rich?'

'Well,' I often say to myself when I think of those words of wisdom, 'It's easy for someone to say such a thing!' Meanwhile, I am here sitting on the side of the road with nothing but holes in my pocket! Yes, I am the lucky one with nothing to lose, as I never had anything in the first place. But looking back, maybe there was some truth in those words of wisdom.

Even if those words fall on deaf ears, there is nothing wrong with that. I guess it is a sign of the times we all live in. Unfortunately, there is no escape from the long arm of destiny, not even from your world. Yes, I am the Beggar of Blackthorn Hill. The last of my kind, living in my world that provides everything my heart desires. A single act of kindness made these two disparate worlds collide, and in the aftermath, an everlasting gift of hope and peace of mind was delivered to all. Striking even the hearts of burdened with suspicion.

When you meet me, you too will wonder, 'How could this be? He must have been chosen by the Gods for such an act. What other reason could it be?' Looking back now, I never had a choice. You would be reading a different story if it was left up to me. But, as I said, all it took was one act of kindness on a night I'll never forget to change everything for all mankind, giving us a new hunger for life so strong not even the wealthy among us could satisfy. Not even for one single day. What was asked of me will deliver a happy ending for all, eternally. But can I be trusted with such a gift? Only you can decide and, maybe in the end, you might even agree that everybody got what they deserved. So, let's begin.

I was very happy in my own little world and never had to share it with anyone. Why should I? I have spent most of my life on the receiving end of everything, which meant one thing to me – getting everything for nothing. I certainly never had anything of value in this world, nor anything that anyone would ever want. It's as simple as that. And do you know why? I'll tell you. Like I said, I'm a beggar, just a simple beggar. What you see is what you get, and I certainly have no frills. I could stick my finger up my nose after a long day and find a sweetener landing in my mouth! And why would I do such a thing? For one simple reason – it's my life, and it's all about me and what I can get for nothing. I have a personality that I can only describe to you as bittersweet, never taking anything for granted. Yes, I am very proud to be a beggar but never confuse me with a tramp. Anyone can fill such shoes.

Truth be told, I am the last of my kind, carrying a lot of mileage on the odometer of my life. I'm an Old Sweat About Town, you might say in a beggar's slang. Not an easy life I've chosen, as it has always been my way or the highway. A beggar only ever has two choices – take it or leave it. And honestly, that's all I ever wanted. I like to think that this life has rewarded me with a sense of freedom that only I can enjoy. There is certainly no point in me trying to explain it to you while I'm in your world. Only my fellow beggars know exactly what I'm talking about. It's a beggar's life. Somebody must do it, and I love it.

Spending most of my time on your worldly streets, begging with no sense of direction, means you could find me anywhere. Well, I like to think I'm gifted with having a great sense of presence; not to worry, I always bow my head to you, so you feel like a king or a queen or whatever your heart desires. But I never bow my head in a sense of shame. Why should I? Often, I only allow the heavenly clouds to take pity upon me and quench my thirst. It's a beggar's life. A great life. And if you are lucky or unlucky enough to cross my palm with silver, you might think that the only simple pleasure you could probably get from me is that I might make you feel a little bit better about yourself – since you have someone to look down on. But that is grand. Like I said, there's no shame in that. After all, is that not the bedrock upon which we all dream?

But I used to wonder if life is that simple for those judging souls who stood over me. Well, it's not. I have learned that there's nothing for nothing in this world, and there is a price for everything, even for a beggar such as me. And you know why? I'll tell you. Most of the time, I get a sense of sadness for those lost souls searching for their peace of mind. The listening watch that I carry within me tells me everything. Who am I going to share their darkest secrets with? Or even what they have for breakfast?

I admit that it's not easy to fall from such grace in this world of yours, but there's no point in me telling such souls there's no shame in that. As I say, 'Was that not when we were at our happiest? When we took our first breath, having nothing, only pride watching over us.' Oh, such pride. This alone has kept me going. But I'd like to stay with you for a while in this world of yours if you'll have me, and I'll explain to you where I'm coming from. My point of view. And trust me when I tell you it's very low as most of the time, I'm sitting in the gutter looking up. This might offer you a better understanding of what it's like to live in my world that gives me everything my heart desires. But for now, all I can do is look at this world of yours with an open mouth. Yes, I must admit this expression always gave me an interesting look on my face. I was never easy on the eye.

It's a hard, old life on the streets. It can be very difficult when you're left-handed in a world that only recognises the right hand of the law. But don't worry, I am a beggar, and I always deliver a false sense of hope like clockwork to the 'do-gooders' as they shower me with gifts while hoping to change my life for the better. Yes, I deliver hope unto them. It's my little gift to this world – a simple pleasure. As I said, I stick my finger up my nose after a long day, a little 'pick me up', in beggar's slang. Yes, such a sweetener, but it's the treasures that I'm craving. I'm hoping for good fortune.

To cross my palm, after all, is that not what makes this world of yours go around? Oh yes, such a prize would be greeted with the utmost gratitude from me. I would rest my hand upon my heart, and it would be just right, perfect, an irresistible spark perching on the high ground and sending them into a trance with a new and fierce fighting spirit. Even I would feel that sticky blessing of wisdom landing upon my shoulders.

Oh, please. Release me from such a society. Only then, when I feel the creaking pain in my jaw, would I take control of the situation by closing my mouth nice and easy. I'd drop a hint and let them know their moment of glory has come and gone, saying, 'Be off with you!'

Yes, it is a hard life on the streets, and the only true value I have is my time. There's a price to be paid for everything. Yes, I would like to think there is some reward for my kind listening ear, you might say, or even for my misery. Trust me when I tell you that often the reality of the situation would arrive, and for a moment of no return, I'd think the penny had dropped – finally, the happy ending I'd been craving. But unfortunately, reality would strike me down with its hidden wall of silence and protect this world of theirs. No place for a beggar such as I.

Like I said, there's a price to be paid for everything. I get nothing, not even a taser, and my only reward is a squinting stare delivered to me as if to say, 'What do you expect?' Oh, those unspoken words. There would be no mistaking it. That crushing blow: how dare I close my mouth? A disgraceful act seen by all, as if to say, 'Let there be no confusion in what status I hold in this world.'

I should be very happy to bask in the company of such wisdom and greatness. 'Never mind,' I'd say to myself. I always make a point of gently stroking my jaw. Wasn't it something to reach for, as if to say there's no such thing as a wasted journey? A simple gesture of hope, I like to think, even for someone like me. After all, I am a shameless beggar blessed with a great presence. Indeed, I am a true master of this world with my silent facial expressions. They alone can speak many languages, understood by whoever stands before me. Such is my power; it can fill the streets with joyful happiness or release such sadness and shame. It can dampen even the brightest of days. Oh, what a gift I carry within! So strong; it brings a tear to my eye. Believe me when I say I am a great beggar for one simple reason – it's all about me. That simple gesture of closing my mouth and breaking the bond to this world. Yes. Give me the power, that fighting edge, that sense of pride in who I am. Yes, and so be it – a disgraceful act seen by all as if I alone, a simple beggar, had released a virus.

I would frequently say to myself, 'I've had enough of this world.' But deep down, a heavy heart of pity would win me over and say, 'Give it another go, beggar. Don't worry about it. It's grand; never mind.' And there's plenty of room in my ear for those unwanted whispers. It's only a matter of time before they look upon me, the beggar of Blackthorn Hill. That's who I am, and many times, I show them the sense of freedom I enjoy with my sharp tongue. Yes, I shout for all to hear. Why not? One disgraceful act as they leave my presence with an unwanted gift of a new spring in their step. You know the type I'm talking about. They have that kind of long-stretching shadow trailing behind them that everyone wants to avoid. It even sends a shiver down my spine. Or maybe they never had love in their lives. Not sure. Whatever it is, they wouldn't be able to hide it from me, no matter how bright the sun shined or how hard the rain pelted down on them. I know them as heavy hearts. You know, I had names for them all. Why not? I had plenty of time on my hands.

Yes, I have to admit, even I got the sneers from them, especially when they stood over me. I don't know why, but they did. They'd be the ones who always overstayed their welcome, even with me. To be honest, I really hated that. Their gaze on me was like a dead weight or a hung jury. And truthfully, most of the time, I'd hear them thinking to themselves. That alone kept me going.

I could always read their shadows, giving me the advantage. If a shadow was wide, it was playful, joyful, and full of merriment. If it was slim, it would be unpredictable and challenging, even for someone like me.

Yes, I could read them all; it's a hidden talent of mine. It's as if I am blessed. But these people all had something in common. They were trying to figure me out – how this poor soul had slipped through the great net of life. Well, let me tell you myself. It's a simple story; what's it to them? From my point of view, they are so wrapped up in the fineries of their own world it might as well be strangling them. The sad thing is, they wouldn't even know it. No thanks. As far as I'm concerned, I'm the lucky one that wiggled through the net. Or maybe it wasn't strong enough to hold me. Whatever. I'd like to think I had a soft landing, you might say. But I always kept my opinion to myself; being outspoken only means one thing to a beggar – empty pockets, no treasures. Too risky, even for someone like me who has nothing to lose and everything to gain. And another thing, while you're here. You'd never know, the next shadow could be the one that changed my life for the better. They're out there, you know. Yes, they could give you everything they have. It's only a matter of time until I get one myself.

I'd like to thank the motherlode of them all. It's a beggar's dream. Hopefully, that will come true one day. And to be honest, it's what I live for while in your world. That alone keeps me going. You never know; it's all about timing, being in the right place at the right time. Timing, that's what they say. Or maybe not. I don't know, and I don't care. But to be honest, I'm not too sure. It's all about looking forward with a sense of pride.

And not to worry, it's fine. If I had choices in my life, I wouldn't change a thing. I'm happy having nothing; I've been used to it since a young lad. But I'll let you in on a little secret of mine – never look up at any of their faces. That was my golden rule. Not an easy one, no matter what would be said to me. I would love to share the sense of freedom I enjoy with my sharp tongue. No, as mentioned, I kept my opinion to myself and let it go over my head. Never look up; one sad face is enough without adding mine to their list, and it could easily drive them out of sight. And I'd get nothing. That's very off-putting for such a beggar as I. And it would be a distraction, even for me. I could easily find myself in a cloud of darkness, questioning myself, 'Am I losing my touch?' All those questions with no answers; you know what I mean. You'd only be letting yourself down with a bang. Yes, I'd like to think I could hold my ground no matter what was said while keeping a sense of pride in my work. And that is another beggar's rule – I have many rules – you never look up into the faces of misery, no matter what. Always keep your eyes down, because very shadow carries a weakness – their shoes. They told me everything about their owners as they towered over me. It's all about the shoes. I love them. Is it a match made in Heaven? Oh, how I can read them as if they were a biography. Yes, another beggar's gift of mine. I know, I am so talented.

You're probably wondering how I ended up on the streets. It's simple. It's my life, and these are the skills that I have mastered over the years. Trust me when I say that I can tell with one glance from my master's beggar's eye if they were wasting my time or not.

As I said, I have given them all names. If they were well-polished, they'd be known as shiny shoes. Which only meant one thing to me – they had plenty of treasures in their pockets despite their inherent tightness. With them, I was never let wanting when it came to free advice, and they would be quite willing to dish it out to me. But if they were well-worn with a bit of mileage under their heels or had lost their shine or looked lived-in, they had their own story to tell. And I know, as spacers only stopping to share in my pain and misery seemingly out of some guilty loyalty to me, as if to say, 'Maybe who I am has something to do with them being a beggar.' Whatever. Nothing more than a simple misunderstanding. Simply mind over matter. I don't mind, so why should it matter? Wise words from a great beggar like me.

Yes, I admit that I am the last of my kind and would take it on the chin. Unfortunately, I'd have to go along with it. In other words, they would be worse off than me and would put on a brave face. They have nothing in their pockets, except pride. But to be fair to them, they would be quite willing to give me something if they had some for themselves. You know it yourself; it would hardly be worth reaching out my hand. But I have a sense of loyalty to them by sharing in their pain. Let them think we're all in it together for a brief moment. Nobody wants to be a busy fool, certainly not me.

I often get the feeling I give more than what I was receiving, but I put that down to the simple lifestyle I live. But then I hear the motherlode approaching – they alone would be worth their weight in gold to me – and all systems go. I call them tappers; you hear them before you see them, giving me the edge to slip my beggar skills into fifth gear and set my trap. There would be no escape from this old sweat. I have a secret weapon that no one could resist; it alone would empty the Bank of England into my pockets. I hear them coming; they have a fear-snapping heel on them, a grip, you might say, on life itself. And they aren't shy of striking the ground with it, lifting themselves above everyone else before coming down for a perfect landing. These would be the shoes I'd be waiting for. A blessing in disguise for one simple reason – they had a hidden touch of class that I love but a weakness that undermines their owners, you might say. It's right underneath their noses, and they can't hide it from me. It's all about the laces. How they were tied. Oh, how I could read them; they always brought the best out of me for one simple reason. Having spent most of their lives on the dusty ground just like me, I could feel a connection with them. It would be my finest moment as a beggar, like a reunion of old friends, a beggar's dream come true as if they were an invitation asking me to take what I want. Just a simple glance out of the corner of my eye. That's all I needed. And only then would I shuffle into a proper position to give myself a little sense of pride in my work. Why not? Then, like love at first sight, game on and over for their master. And the laces would never get entangled with their masters and the finer things of life, no, I'm glad to see they're nothing more than simple victims of their own success. It was my body language, a silent strength, my beggar's eye, that was the final strike. A little twinkle of it that nobody could resist but could make or break me, so it had to be just right. To be fair, my timing was always perfect. This all depended on how the laces were tied, such as if they had a tight knot with a bow. Then, they were sticking to their budget, meaning they had already decided what treasures I was going to ge and I had to be quick and snappy, no tears. Like we were two professionals negotiating a contract. But if they were loosely tied, dangling all over the place, then there was room for manoeuvring, and I could bargain for a lot more treasures than I should.

Like I said, it all depended on my beggar's eye; timing was everything in that minute. See the hand slipping into the pocket, searching for that hidden treasure. Let them have it. Fully blessed, then take them down. No mercy would be shown, just a little slice of an uppercut, as if saying, 'What you are giving me is the difference between life and death.' And only after, when I hear that magic silence of the hidden hand searching, did it mean that I had them hooked.

With my beggar's eye, it was perfect timing and a knockout. I had them in the palm of my hand, and I received a lot more than I should. It was always down to my beggar's eye, perfect every time, like magic with its fraction-of-a-second timing. Like I said, it had to be just right. Not too short, not too long. If it was too short, you'd be sending out signals, and it could be seen as a lack of respect. And if you dragged it out, it gave the impression you wanted to go home with them, God forbid. No. It had to be short and sweet, just right – the beggar's touch. And they loved it as if I had given them the magical power to change my life from misery to happiness. Even I would celebrate by resting my hand on my chest, signalling that what they have given me will change my life for the better. But, like I said, it would be nothing more than a false hope for all. Soon enough they'd be off, clicking their heels with a sense of pride. Well, it all depended on who was watching them, who never let their side down, as if to see they were enjoying the company of a beggar. You know yourself, anyway, I wouldn't blame them. It's my life, and it's all about the misery.

That's where the treasures are for me, and it has nothing to do with happiness. There's no room for that type of thing. Happiness, for one simple reason, would be bad for business. It's all about me, isn't it? And what I can get for nothing. It's just the sign of the times we live in – every beggar for himself. Isn't it grand? I like to think that whatever treasures I get were a fair exchange of goods. At least we all got something out of it. Yes, I like to think I am a great beggar. Well, what I'm trying to say is, in a nutshell, before I do anything for anyone, I always see what was in in for me. Now, isn't that simple, even for a beggar with nothing to lose? That always kept me on the path of riches. Yes, it's hard to believe that someone like me could hold the balance of power and change everything for these two worlds we live in, and no one saw it coming. Not even I. And maybe, now, we live our lives in a better place. I don't know; it all depends on the world you live in. Only you can decide for yourself.

Chapter 2

The Rain

I love the rain; it always made me happy for one simple reason. I could hide within full view of everyone. Nobody in their right mind would ever stand around in the rain and stare at me. It made me fit into society for as long as the downpour lasted.

Yes, I've been told I have a very short attention span. I've been told It had something to do with a lack of education. Now, speaking for myself, I felt it had nothing at all to do with it. The only education I needed was learning to be in the right place at the right time just in case I missed something. Especially if it was going for nothing – a hand-me-out, as I said. I loved it when the heavens opened; it always presented me with an opportunity. And, of course, being a beggar, I couldn't let it pass. With nothing to lose, I would take full advantage of the situation.

Shelter would be on everybody's mind when it rained. It made no difference who or what you were; shelter was the magic word. Oh, the rain – a curse to them and a blessing to me. But I would be in no rush for my shelter. I would stand in the rain for as long as it took until I spotted the right type of crowd seeking shelter. In other words, there had to be something interesting about them. Ideally, they were well-groomed, as if they had something to offer society or had a bit of pride in themselves. I looked for grandeur. Yes, that's it – grandeur. I've never had it, but I like the sound of it. That's what would catch my eye. I'd be looking for an air of importance and grandeur; well, that's what they say makes this world go round. I'd be looking for that, and where better to find it than in a crowd taking shelter? That's the best place to find such a thing as grandeur or respectability. I think so. And I'd want some of it for myself. It costs nothing; the smell of it alone would be worth it. The only way of getting this grandeur was to take shelter with the newly selected group I had chosen and blend in.

I like to think we all have something in common. All I had to do was make my way over; they never even saw or heard me. The rain was a perfect cover, as if it had that magic power to make this world more approachable, dropping its guard just for a few precious moments. As my listening watch would tell me, the crowd's silent lips gaped amongst themselves, 'How could the heavens have opened in this world of theirs, trapping them?' They lost that sense of freedom and entitlement they had taken for granted. I love it – the rain – because we share a common ground of unpredictability. And before they know it, I am within in their ranks, and I make my move and say with a deep voice as I try to mimic their grandeur, 'Well, what's the story?' And wait for the magic moment to arrive.

It's a downpour without even a hint that there was a beggar among them. That's what I'd be waiting for, as I cast my gaze up in the air, thinking, 'Thank you for the rain and for recognising me as having a voice. I've only ever wanted to be heard.' And it certainly didn't matter if this world wanted me or not. I didn't care; the job was done. It would be worth its weight in gold since I knew the position I held in this world. I was at the very bottom of the pile. It couldn't get any worse for me, even if a stranger came to town with nothing to offer anyone; I'm sure he'd be more interesting than me. But, like I said, I didn't care. I suppose there's no one to blame except myself. But for those brief seconds, the rain provided me a new circle of friends that I could enjoy in silence.

But when they get a whiff that there is a beggar amongst their ranks, you could hear those faint little voices taking control of the situation with a whisper. Releasing it into the crowd, the circle is beginning to lighten. 'I'm off,' one would say, and another would say, 'I think I'll take a chance.' 'You're right,' yet another one would say, 'I'll go for it.' And they would be off, leaving me to think that if I had someplace important to go, then I'd also be off.

Oh, how I hated being last. I don't know why. I've never been first. I just wanted to be in the middle. Nothing wrong with that. But if I could get away first just once in my beggar's life, it would mean so much to me. Then I'd be important; last was never any good, not even for me. It's like being the leftovers, the scraps upon the plate, or the crumbs that had fallen to the ground that nobody wanted – that's what it meant to me. You know what I mean? But I always waited until the end; I knew my place in this world, no matter what.

Left standing with one stranger, I could see from their twitching face they are busy planning thier escape from me. They have that kind of wandering eye that I would follow, but I would hang on for dear life for those few extra seconds as if they were letting me know it had nothing to do with me. They didn't want to hurt my feelings by leaving me on my own. It didn't matter; it was fine. I'm a tough old beggar, but I always give them the way out. And I say, 'We'd better go for it; there could be another downpour.' Then they say, 'Yes, I'll see you,' and they are off, leaving me standing there, thinking about what was said to me. 'I'll see you.' Maybe it's a hidden message to me, as if to say, 'Until we meet again,' or maybe, 'I'll see you as long as you don't see me.' All I know is that it won't take long before all those thoughts of grandeur will be washed away into the gutter where they belong and all this was nothing more than a walk-through, a talk-through. Yes, I really do have to apologise for the rain. It certainly isn't to everyone's taste, and I say to myself, 'Let's get on with it, beggar. It's your life, and this world waits for no one.'

Then, 'But wasn't it worth it?' I say to myself, as their scents linger with me for most of the day. I know it's my fault; I've heard it many times. But that's the way I live my life. I can't help it. This is the price I have to pay for my freedom. And maybe my life would be a lot different if I had corrected everyone when they pointed and said, 'Look, there's the beggar of Blackthorn Hill.'

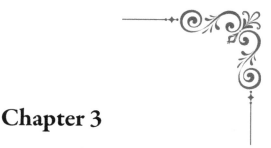

Chapter 3

The Window

Oh, how I love to scurry around the streets of your world, lurking within the shadows and appearing wherever I want with my cap in hand. I have my favourite spots to set up camp for a few hours. Not because of the treasures those places have to offer, but because of the interesting people. I love watching them; it costs nothing. How they carry themselves and pretend not to see me, but I catch them out with a wink from my eye. Oh, the horror upon their faces from such a brief interaction. But they never smile. Yes, they are always making a statement to the world, showing how they should be seen.

As my choice of colour is always black – I love black – I like to think I am always in fashion, no matter what season we're in. Especially considering some wear nothing at all, given half a chance. What a strange world this is, even through the eyes of a beggar. But never mind; I don't tend to linger in my camps. I would be off to more familiar hunting grounds. Well, what I'm trying to say is that I eventually feel a little bit peckish, in beggar's language – a free meal. It wouldn't take long to get one, given my great presence. Before I know it, I would be uptown, gazing into a large window where a lot of fine dining was going on. It was a very simple affair; if I could see them feasting on the finer things life had to offer, they could certainly see me.

It didn't take long before the beggar magic got a grip on the place. I was spotted with sets of roaming eyes. A distraction, especially when they're eating. But I hung in there and wait for the slight tilting of their hand in my favour. Eventually, with a mighty struggle, they rested their eating tools before their time. The only comfort they could enjoy was resting their chin upon the palm of their hand and trying to hide that fine swallow of shame. But not to fear, they'd fight back with a snappy clicking sound of their fingers, summoning their helping hands and arriving, hot and bothered in all their glory, without delay. Yes, I would be spotted – the focal point of attraction. And only then would I finish them off by opening my mouth as wide as I could, releasing a misty cloud of desperation – a simple message of hunger. Well, I like to think it brought out the best in people as I would be quickly handed a bag of goodies with the unspoken command, 'Away with you, beggar.' Yes, it cost nothing – only a private sitting for me that was out of sight, out of mind. Yes, I like to think of it as mutual respect that satisfied all parties in this world of plenty. And there's no shame in that.

If truth be told, I have my ups and downs like everybody else. And if I wanted a lift in life, there was only one place known to me as Paradise Corner. But to all in this world it was simply the bottle bank, arriving in the middle of the night like a drunken lord with its swollen belly and plonking itself down while never refusing another drink – a gift from this world to me. Yes, I hear it calling to me many times. A cheers to all in celebration with a tipple of red or white, whichever your heart desires. Or stay within the middle classes and try every flavour at once.

Before I knew it, I gain the power to lose track of time, as if the hours of the day all rolled into one. And no matter what was said, I could give take it back. Yes, I would be blinded out of my mind with such dazzling colour like I was hitching a ride on a rainbow through the passages of time, searching for a happy ending. Yes, it would be a trip of a lifetime that didn't need any baggage. As I often heard, 'It's the key to all happiness.' Even if I had such riches, I'd have no one to share it with since most of the shops were closed and locked.

I'd see to you when I came to your door. First, though, I'd look through the keyhole with my listening watch and enjoy the sounds of good fortune and happiness it brought everyone. It would be grand – even for me. I, too, would have captured the magic of its silent display, with everything good and wonderful this world has to offer. And it didn't matter if there was room for me or not. Sometimes, I would try to hide in such happiness for everyone to see. But I always looked away or took a step back, knowing in my heart that such a display was never for me.

Yes, there was to be no escape from who I am – the beggar of Blackthorn Hill. But not to worry. Even I have a place in this world. Yes, the beggar's bench that was hidden away on the side of a street like time itself had forgotten. No one would ever dare sit upon it for one simple reason – it's mine. Even my name is scratched into such a bench. Most days, it wouldn't take long when I would be shuffled into position alongside my pigeon friends. I knew them all – large and small, old and young. We were the best of friends, having an unspoken trust between us. A certain respect gained over the years that announced, 'What you see is what you get.' I like to think of it like having a safe pair of hands. They'd land within my open palms, tilting their heads to me. Most of all, they had that magic in them that brought this forgotten place back to life. It lifted my spirit to new dizzy heights and I'd tell them many times, 'I couldn't imagine my life without you.' Our friendship always gave me a sense of status. You might say we were all in a pecking order. But I never sat among them. Each to our own. Why not? Having a mutual respect for all our boundaries, as if I, the beggar of Blackthorn Hill, was the chosen one. As if they would perch themselves on my shoulder, sharing with them a sense of suspicion and knowing where there was a window or an eye. You never know who is watching.

When I got a quiet moment, I closed my eyes and drift away into my world, which gave me a hidden strength to carry on. It's all I ever needed in my life to keep me going in this world of plenty where nothing is real – this power to live in the past, the present, and even the future. But it couldn't last long, as I'm rudely interrupted by someone shouting from a distance, 'Beggar, look what I have for you!' It's the voice of reality, arriving in all its glory and clipping my wings to drop me back to earth. Not even giving me those few precious seconds of happiness to enjoy or stealing a moment in time; it's gone, lost in this world of theirs. I'm grounded, taking a deep breath and opening my eyes with a slanting kind of a look. If only I could spread my wings like my feathered friends and take flight and enjoy the freedom.

'What is this great treasure you have got for me that's so important?' I asked, dazzled by a large set of white sparkling teeth looking down on me. Yes, it was one of those days where there was no escape. I started to straighten my face and focus my eyes, hoping to build a sense of excitement along the way. As I said, it's all part and parcel of being a professional beggar. Well, I couldn't help it. I had to have whatever was on offer no matter what. It was all part of the job, I wondered what it could be – a head-turner? Such self-importance to interrupt my perfect escape. A sandwich appeared out of nowhere, only inches from my face. Well wrapped and protected from the elements – nearly ready to eat.

'Yes, there's a sense of love within their hands,' I thought as I glance at its beholder. Yes, I saw a house of love in their hands and wonder if I had a little bit more wrapping when I was a young lad then I, too, could be loved in this world. Or maybe this is the price of happiness. 'No thanks, I'm fine, thanks all the same,' I said and closed my eyes, thinking I might be able to make it back to the dizzy heights of happiness. No. It was gone. Those voices inside my head wouldn't let me go. 'Take it, beggar. It's who you are – a beautiful sandwich. It would make your health.' I raised my eyes in the darkness beneath my lids, thinking, 'It's always very simple – what I see is what I eat.' Like I mentioned, it's just the beggar in me. I only have two choices – take it or leave it. I could surrender to those hands of determination towering over me, picking me up. I could easily spend the whole day feeding the pigeons with such a prize. Or I'd place it in my pocket with a new sense of pride instead of a dead weight of pity or shame that had no value to me. A sense of gratitude would be exchanged between us with a nod from our heads. 'Yes,' I said to myself, 'Time to get the ball rolling; time for action.' I thought this as I got myself into fifth gear. After all, I had a job to do. All I had to do was to remove my shoes.

There was something about not having shoes in this world of ours. The act held such power that it could put everybody into a panic, sending a cold shiver down their backs. And it wouldn't take long before my begging bowl would be singing out of tune with treasures. And I'd have a new pair of shoes landed at my feet like I was royalty with a silent tilting of approval to see if I'd take them. So, if they insist, I slip them on for all to see and gift them a thumbs-up, as if to say, 'Perfect fit.' And we're back in business. And if the truth be told, I hated shoes. I could never figure out which one fit on which foot. I am always putting them on the wrong way around. But it doesn't matter; it's grand. I've never worn them in my world.

Chapter 4

The School Bell

When I hear the school bell, it is the sound young dreams are made of. Having nothing to offer, I stand aside as the early morning trickle of little people passes me, carrying their school bags packed with dreams and hope that help them face the misty morning sun. They stare at me, only to be pulled along with a mother's love, hoping for a better life. As I sneak a wink at them, oh, the shock of it all as they try to look away while keeping an eye of suspicion upon me. A young leader stands and shouts out for all to hear, 'Well, beggar, how's it going?' He looks to his followers in a way that conveys that they made the right choice when picking him. But it's always a joy to hear them laugh and sing along with no strings attached, knowing that life is still a fairy tale and in no hurry to end. Yes, they lift the misty morning even for an old beggar such as myself, allowing me to dream until the street falls quiet again.

The peace is interrupted by a little figurine with dangling shoelaces – his innocence catches my beggar's eye. He makes his way along his chosen path while testing its verges for danger, one foot in front of the other, without even looking. But I see the speeding carriages of death trying to clip his heels. Its master speaks a blinding feast of words to its invisible friends. I jump to my feet and take that almighty step, thinking my presence alone will surely be strong enough to catch even the laziest of eyes. And only then do they come to a screeching stop of anger. Its master stares at me with challenging eyes but only bows its head in shame to let him pass.

'Oh, beggar,' he says to me, 'Could you tie my shoelaces?' I look into his eyes and can see his fairy tale is well and truly over. I drop to my knees and tie his laces as tight as I can to try and keep him safe in this world in some small way. We share a smile that says, 'Maybe it's okay to dream again.' Our eyes catch the robin landing on my bench. It serenades us. 'Well,' I say to my feathered friend, 'Your mother must have forgotten to tell you shouldn't chirp to strangers.' As it flies away, I tell the boy, 'Now, my little man, you'd better follow him, as I'm sure you'll be missed.' Just like that little robin, off he goes with a little whisper to me, 'Thank you, beggar. You're so kind.'

This is a very special occasion, making me feel I had some value even in this world of theirs. Even though I've never answered the toll of the school bell, I thank God for those good deeds. They can appear out of nowhere just like a robin, especially when you're not looking. Then the town clock strikes one, and I look to the sky as a startling of crows take flight, a gripping hunger for darkness in their form. With every strike of the clock's heavy hand of time, the streets fill with such greed and pushes me to one side. Upon the hour, I am not wanted. I had to get out and let them fight for their lives. I had to flee; a sensation overpowered me like I am beginning to lose my freedom.

My freedom is the one thing I always had in my life, separating my existence from this world. I gather myself and make my escape. After all, I wouldn't be missed since nobody ever searches the shadowy streets for a beggar such as myself. So, yes, I'm off, bags and all resting upon my shoulders and leaving nothing. Only a secreting trail of dust rises behind me and covers my tracks. I never look behind me, no matter what whispers might be chasing me. There's no point. The fear of losing my sense of freedom always keeps me on the right path. But I never leave this world of plenty without gathering all these falling stars. They come crashing down from ancient oak trees of wisdom, searching this land of stone for a new beginning. I'm the beggar after all. I always rescue them from such a fate, placing them within my pocket, leaving nothing of value except an empty shell.

I only stop in my escape to raise my hand with a smile to my dear old friend. She is an elderly lady who lived between these two worlds. 'The Witch,' they call her. She carries an arch upon her back and wears red lipstick to lift the colour of death from her face. She never takes her eyes off the ground, telling me once that she had seen enough in front of her to last a lifetime.

'Well, beggar,' she says in a determined voice, 'how many falling stars did you save today?' Her shivery eyes are firmly fixed upon the palm of my hand. 'Plant them, my beggar, in your world. May their roots have a deep grip on life itself. It will be a reminder to all that even goodwill can allude decay for a thousand years.' As I bury my treasures at her feet, she asks, 'Did we get anything interesting today, my beggar? Let's see.' Something catches her eye and she points to it with her stick like a great guardian of these two worlds making a final decision. She says to me, 'I don't think you have any use for such a thing in your world, beggar.'

'You're probably right. I'll leave it.' So, I give it to her. 'You have a heart of gold, my beggar. It's a pity no one knows its true value.' But my eye catches a glimmer of hope even in the darkness of night. As if telling me to take such glitter to the perfect resting place and bring joy to all. Knowing when I get to the end of my path that my load will be a lot lighter than what I started out with. Usually, I try to hang on for dear life to such treasures even knowing I have to surrender and let them go. But when all is said and done, it would be a welcome break even for me. I could rest in peace amongst the dead, having their own story to tell. It would be chiselled in stone for all to see. A sense of pride even for those who would have departed before their time. There would be nothing left. Just dreams of what could have been. They always found me very interesting and never dreamt of interrupting me.

Yes, I would capture all the magic with such treasures, chiming within the wind and setting a tone like a sweet lullaby for all. May they rest in peace and never forget the candle's flickering light as if to say, 'There was always a glimmer of light, even amongst the dead.' And then I'd find my one true love that gave me the greatest gift of all – life. A mist of rain would fall upon my cheeks, hiding my tears of sorrow and joy, just as life itself taught me. Acceptance is always so gracious, even in the darkest of hours.

As this shadowing world begins to fade into the evening dusk, I have no fear since I hear my world calling, 'Beggar? Beggar, where are you?' And that's where I go, with nothing beyond my memories of the day. But I always fall upon my knees at the edge of my world, cradling that new sense of life with a helping hand to reach for the sky. That glimmer of hope of a watchful eye, just like how my father once gazed upon me. I, too, would scratch this world and place those fallen stars within. Yes, taking their rightful place in this great world of mine. I rise up amongst splendour as far as the eye can see, and always protect this world of mine with its shadowed past.

Yes, this is my world. All mine. It's certainly a different existence in this world of mine. As I said, there are no frills and everything you see is mine and mine alone. I love it for one reason – I am king. I could never imagine my life without such a place. We belong together; I'm reminded as I always stop and listen to its gentle whispering wind in my ear that tells me everything. There would be no stone left unturned and it always welcomed me home, saying, 'Oh, beggar, we missed you so much.' What can I say? How could I ever want anything more in my life? We have it – an unconditional love for who we are. And, certainly, we don't have any concerns or interests for anything that lives within our shadow. And you know why? Because they're soft. They have an internal weakness for the finer things in life. It takes a great person, such as a beggar like myself, to live here. It's my world, and if you don't like it, then get out and stay out. You were never wanted. It's my way or the highway for anyone in my world. Yes, I am certainly the chosen one.

Oh, the voices within bless me even with such a name as beggar. And if you're looking for me in my world, guess what? You'll find me, no problem. There's no getting the wrong beggar. I'm the only beggar here amidst such splendour and beauty. Master and king of all. That's me – the beggar of Blackthorn Hill. And if you're looking for me, well, I don't know why you would be. But if you're here – avoiding a long story or history lesson – you'll find me straight away. And if anyone was too proud to say my name aloud, a simple gesture of raising your sniffling nose would reveal my direction. Trust me when I tell you there'll be no mistake. I'll be there at the end of it with my listening watch.

Yes, this might seem to everyone as some shameful isolation. So be it; there's no helping it. Oh, those voices within tell me, 'Never mind, it's a small price to pay for such happiness.' But when I get a quiet moment, I'd say to myself, 'It's grand. Don't worry about it. It's how I live my life.'

Oh, please. Forgive me for saying such a thing. Even I get a little bit confused when I hear those voices within, telling me how to act or the right thing to do. I could never figure it out. Or maybe they just enjoy their lives at my expense. But I do feel a sense of excitement. It's been a long time since I had such company. Since you are in my world, hopefully you can stay a while with me. Besides, what's the hurry? Time is on your side. Nothing's planned. You may even say to yourself, 'How did I become a beggar?' Well, it's like this – see, I certainly didn't come from a long line of family beggars.

Chapter 5

Beggar's Name

I became a beggar out of pure love from my mother during long-past happier times. She would smile and say to me, 'If I didn't know you, I'd think you're a little beggar boy.' Especially when I came into the house after a long day rooting and tearing on the side of the hill. But with time, the boy grew up and left behind nothing but a beggar with a legacy of hand-me-downs. Those things never held any value for their original owners, but in some small way they formed a foundation for me. But that didn't matter to me. Like I said, I was born with nothing, and that's all I've ever needed to live in this world. Yes, lucky me, free from a world full of trappings, allowing me to live my life without standards. Everything was up for grabs. Even as a young fella, I would start the day with nothing and be loaded up by nightfall. In my eyes, there was no shame taking things from people. I couldn't get enough; I wanted everything even if I didn't need it. I had to have it like some compulsion. Things would be shoved into my palms, and when my hands were full, I would carry them in my mouth. I left nothing. I would be told, 'Now, little man, say nothing to no one. It's all yours.' I loved hearing those words; it made me feel like I was the chosen one in some epic. Yes, all mine. Even for me it was so refreshing. I would convey a sense of gratitude with a nod of my head followed by a wink of my eye, as if to say, 'See, it's all about me.'

But that was then. This is now. So, let's move on and not dwell too much on the past. Let's stay ahead of the evening twilight. It would be wise since my fate has already been decided. Just like the changing colours of the autumn leaves, it is what it is in my world. There's no changing them, and it doesn't even matter what time or space they live in. The great hand of nature is the master of all seasons. It's all about the bigger picture regarding life. And trust me when I tell you that you can only influence nature; you will never beat it. And I must say, I am living proof of this. My life so far has been just one long day with no beginning and no end in sight. I have been gifted with such an expansive sense of time that it is impossible to enjoy. I live for the moment like the great trees of wisdom that tie their roots together and live as one. I watch the days slip away and wait for the arrival of another with a sense of excitement as if every day is a celebration. It brings with it the gift of a new life like those falling stars I planted in the soil of Blackthorn Hill. They grow and shape their lives with the sunrise; they bow their heads to me with every sunset for giving them the greatest gift of all – a helping hand in their hour of need. Yes, it's like a new life for all in my world. For some, they might never see another day, and only then would I surrender to the nightfall gripping your world. Yes, I'm ashamed to say that even a beggar like me has a weakness for your world.

Every day, I find a spot that gives me a full view of your world as you all race around and search for a new sense of purpose. Underneath the covers of darkness, I always gaze at the night sky where the stars twinkle at me as if they were saying, 'Are we not the lucky ones? Always having our rightful place, no matter what shadows would be hanging over us?' Yes, I belong to Blackthorn Hill, gifting me a great sense of freedom and telling me how to live my life. Maybe even giving me a right to enjoy what life has to offer. It always gave me the choice if I wanted to enjoy it or let go, sealing away its magic for another time. But when all is said and done, I wouldn't change a thing. Like I said, I was born into it. It's who I am. What would I do with myself if I could? I might end up exposed for all to see, just like the displays in the shop window. Well, I am a beggar, after all. I must never forget. It's all about me and that sense of freedom I enjoy. It is that simple. I never had to worry about life and what it had to offer me. I like to think I'm simply passing through. I could do what I wanted. I could even travel to the moon. There was never any concern for me. And if somebody questioned or even enquired about the beggar of Blackthorn Hill - what was he doing, where was he going, or even complained – they would be told, 'He's just a beggar, don't worry about it. And besides, what's it to you?' That would bring all inquiries to a snappy end.

That's the line I like to think should never be crossed. Our two worlds must remain separated, and in return, I'd never find myself in a situation in your world that I couldn't walk away from. Even if it was my last day on this Earth, 'God forbid,' I would say to myself, 'I was one lucky beggar.' Lucky because I was happy with a great life, and, better still, knew I would be resting on the shoulders of strangers for free. They would be delivering me to a better life. How mad is that? Isn't that a simple price for such freedom? But life is like flicking a coin into the air, even for me. There are always two sides to every story. But it's the side I never saw coming that changed everything. But why is it me? After all, I'm just a beggar with nothing to offer. And there's nothing in your world that I want, not even contained within the dizzying heights you call knowledge. You like to believe it provides you a great position of authority, even though it might never let you rest. I've seen many times how you would have enough and you would still try to end it all by your own hand as you lay on the street with nothing, waiting with eyes closed only to say, 'Please release me.' I'm sure tongues would be wagging in the wrong direction. Or maybe it's just when no one cares that it's freedom.

So there you have it, my opinion of a world that never sleeps. I can tell you one thing, the only company I enjoy is the gentle shuffling sound of the thorny briars. They seem to reach out to me and say, 'We have you, beggar.' Yes, I have to admit, it's unconditional love that has always guarded this path leading to my world. Whoever dares to enter uninvited will be ripped to shreds without mercy. Now, is that not love so strong it causes heartburn? 'Yes, we do look after each other up here,' I say to myself. There will be no visitors this night; there never are. But it's nice, right? Who cares? Well, I'd like to think no matter what, my beggar's door is always open for certain souls. Even if I was blinded by a celebration from your world, have no fear. The scented wild roses always bring me to my front door even in the darkest of nights. Yes, I like to think this large shack home. And don't be shy; come along. I live alone; you have nothing to fear. Kicking off my shoes, they go flying in every direction because that job was done in your world. The shoes have nothing to offer me in my world except carrying within them an element of suspicion and shame.

I never wear such shoes in my world since it would be insulting, a lack of respect for what lies underfoot. Well, what I'm trying to say is we share a hidden depth of trust between us. It's as if we are one. And no matter what danger lies at my feet, not a single drop of blood would be split between us. Yes, we look after each other up here. It's our way. But while you're here, I want to tell you about the stone of death that rests beneath my feet, like a welcome mat that harbours a dark secret. It's better known as the Hangman's Step. In other words, the last solid piece of ground many poor souls stood on before meeting their maker. And here it lies at my front door for one simple reason – I got it for nothing. It was decided that it would be given to me, the beggar of Blackthorn Hill, because I have nothing to lose. But to me, it is a perfect fit in my world, because we share a common ground. It is what it is, and there is never any wiggle room when steeping upon it as if your hands were tied behind your back. It always gives me a sensation of never having a choice in life or death. Yes, there was no return from such a fate when stepping upon it. Not even for me. But I love it all the same. And when I've had enough of such torment, I open my eyes and see the light. I step away from it and live to tell the tale with a smile on my face. Yes, I am a great beggar, so maybe I can even cheat death. With nothing to lose, maybe you'd like to try? Or is it a step too far for you? Trust me, it makes the world different, knowing you had a lucky escape from such a fate. Or maybe it's nothing more than an opportunity for me to cheat death every day of my life. Yes, I stand on this cold stone of death and face my world. I scream and shout 'Who am I, filling this world of mine with such a question?' Only it can answer, and I wait in silence for its echo calling back to me, the beggar of Blackthorn Hill, 'We are one, forever and ever.' Yes, I'm home alone for all to hear. Well, I might have unwanted visitors like my four-legged friends. I always give them the element of surprise to scatter; they love that kind of thing, the wildness of it all. But to me, it's home sweet home. There's nothing like it as everything here has been frozen in time. I like it that way. Even the old clock on the wall stopped when it reached its prime, enjoying the last seconds. It could never find the right time to let it go. But it still conjures a silent stillness of excitement within me since I never know when it could strike me. Perhaps only I could enjoy such a terror. Yes, I was never alone in this world of mine, which always gives me a sense of calmness. After your world, it's a respite from a life sentence of noise. Yes, this place is cold to the touch. It never gets too hot – just right. It carries with it an unforgiving justice even if you were feeling under the weather. But it's perfect for a beggar such as me.

And before I know it, I'm in my chair of solid ash as I gaze upon the fire. 'Look what I've got for you,' I say. And then, the sparks fly with a sense of excitement when I open the bag of goodies and share my stories with those burning flames. 'Wait until I tell you about those shoes.' Yes, these would be the ones that would have saved the little lost soul from the carriages of death. Into the fire with them. I wait for the magic of the blue flame to rise and greet me and search it for his little face of happiness. I find it glowing with a sense of pride as if to say, 'Well done, beggar. That was a great story.' And only then would I reach over the flames for the kettle as black as the ace of spades – it had a hidden, silent strength within it. It was happy to sit and wait for the beggar's hand; I would tilt it when the time is right, and it was in my favour. Its boiling water would reward me with a nice jam jar of tea. That was the one true love in my life. I loved it.

Chapter 6

Hidden Treasures

———— ⚬❧⚬ ————

I loved those jam jars of tea. I could drink them all day, all night, as every jam jar had a different taste. Why not? When I put one down, I could never remember where or even how find it. It was just one of those things. Maybe it was because I was left-handed. If I were right-handed, my life could be a lot different. Oh, those voices would always come to my rescue. They'd tell me it was just a simple misunderstanding. Why should I care? They'd remind me I was just a beggar. But there was never any shortage of jam jars in my world. Now and again, I'd have a little help from sweet-tasting busy bees hovering around. They delighted in taking full advantage of my misfortune and steal from such a sweet-tasting treasure. Never mind, it was okay. Finders' keepers.

I stretched out my legs and glanced at my toes, saying to myself, 'They're like sets of wrought-iron pokers, straight and black. As you know, a house is only as good as its foundation. They're doing their job.' My toes were crowned with a set of curled nails that had such a grip on my world as if they were anchors that never let me slip, unlike some I have seen. They were like a crowd climbing the stairs all at once and going nowhere. Yes, these toes of mine are worth their weight in gold. I would be lost without them. I wiggle them as if to say, 'Who do you love? Are we not all in this together for better or for worse?'

Well, like I said, I had the freedom to do whatever I wanted and spoke the hidden truth that nobody wanted to hear. Yes, the renowned sharpness of a beggar's tongue. I couldn't help it, even though it resulted in nothing except isolation for me. Yes, my name gave me the gift of free speech. Many times, I would think maybe such a price is too high, even for me. I would often rest my face in my hands if only to see if it still fit into this world of mine. Maybe I should just be like those falling stars and place my trust in the hands of a stranger and wait for a new life to begin. Oh well, there is no changing me now. Yes, I'm very lucky because everyone knows me. Even people I have never met before. They'd point to me and say, 'Look, the beggar of Blackthorn Hill.' I would often wave my hand into the air with a sense of pride for who I am. I'd be trying to catch their eye, but it always seemed to be in vain. They always ended up rushing away. I only ever wanted to say hello; there's no harm in that. It don't cost nothing.

Such thoughts make me a bit peckish. I put my hand in my pocket; I always have a steady supply of goodies. A treat it would be; I never know what could appear. Well, in a nutshell, I always find something to eat. I could discover anything from a floppy sandwich to a soggy biscuit in hand. I rest it by the fire, smacking my hands as I watch it turn golden brown – a feast fit for a king. With a quick sniffle of my nose, I gobble it down. As usual when there was a bit of crust left, I flick it over my shoulder to my little four-legged friends in a gesture that lets them know that what goes around comes around in this world of mine. What more could a beggar want out of life? A simple plan, even for a beggar like me. But little did I know, this would be the last time I'd have peace of mind. Everything was about to change. Even the voices within were set to challenge me. Yes, changes were afoot for all. Destiny had decided it was time to enter my world. It did so with a blinding, glittering light that blazed across my eye. I quickly closed it, but somehow it had migrated to the other one. What could it be? I realised it lay at my feet, not in my eye. It must have fallen to the ground from my pocket. A little gift just for me. Who would do such a thing? Maybe it's the little chap of insanity that lives his life on the verge of danger. He must have placed it in my pocket. It had to be him.

I crouched down and took a closer look. It was a picture of me, all battered and bruised, as if I, the beggar of Blackthorn Hill, was carrying the weight of their world upon my shoulders. Yet, it had such a sparkle within it, like the me in the photograph was surrounded by all the colours of the rainbow. I tenderly held it like a newborn in the palm of my hand. Even though it came from a world blinded by greed, it had been a long time since I got something out of kindness rather than pity. Indeed, it was a great treasure that would always stand the test of time, even for me. If this kind soul could reach out into my world, maybe someday I could reach into his. But for now, I settled on a bench outside under the tree of knowledge. I've never called it a night without sitting outside on a wooden bench. We were the best of friends despite what life itself had thrown at us. We always rested quite peacefully underneath this great tree of knowledge. To me, its strength was always in its silence regardless of what it heard. Its branches, reaching for the sky, had such strength in them.

Yes, it's a great spot of mine to sit and gaze upon the magic of the night sky. I've never had to wish upon a star. I've always known; I had this great tree of knowledge as a reminder of who I am and where I belong. I place my hands upon its trunk and listen to its gentle quaking. 'Yes,' I thought, 'You are the master of all time and everything within. I really do welcome you to my world. If you are willing to walk in my footsteps, trust me when I tell you that at the end of this beggar path, you will always smile and think of me. Life really is just like one long day of happiness.' But, like I said, I never saw it coming. Hopefully, we're all in the right frame of mind seeing as this is the point of no return – not even for you.

This was the hour of need for all. Well, this was the day when one act of kindness changed everything for me. In return, I was gifted by the great hand of Mother Nature a new life that was ruthless loyal to me. This loyalty decided the existence of our two worlds. Looking back on it now, it was a match made in heaven. All I had to do was light that spark. Trust me when I tell you, our fate was in the hands of a beggar that night. You know what that means? Or what was in it for me? Nothing – there was in your world that I could ever want.

There was nothing unusual about the arrival of that day, only the sounds of me breaking wind in a high tone - entirely dependent on what I consumed the night before. I waved my hand across my face and feel the strength of it. After it passed, I faced a new day without ever having the distraction of having a set of fluttering butterfly eyes gazing into mine. Certainly not; no time for that. This is a beggar's life, and I'm glad to just hear the angry voices in my head, screaming and shouting all at once while trying to make their escape from such a calling.

My two-legged friend, the cock I called Cock, tended to perch on my tree of knowledge as he perfected his morning call at my expense. He never allowed me a lie-in, eventually mastering his call. Maybe that's why the tree of knowledge is known for its silence because it couldn't get a word in with that deafening sound from this fellow. There he'd be, looking right down into my bedroom window and giving me the full blasting sound of perfection. Yes, that perfect note would ring endlessly in my ears. It was the only one he could sing, but he was blessed with a great pair of lungs. He wouldn't stop until I stuck my head out of my bedroom window and made a kind of hissing sound, letting him know, 'Any chance you could turn it down so we could have a bit of normality on the hill?' Only then would he tilt his head and give me a certain look as they said, 'I'm an early bird, just doing my job. It is what it is.' What a crazy world I live in; it can have such quirkiness.

I could hear a pin drop. It was that type of place. But to be totally honest with you, I always looked up to Cock. I admired him. He had certain qualities that I always lacked. In particular, I've never been any good in the morning. It was down to my lifestyle; there was no sense of time in my world, and everyone knew this. The days often ran into the nights and the nights stretched like a week. But this is my world.

Although, it would be nice for him if he had a life outside his work and took a page out of my book. To be honest, I don't know how the hens live with him. They were probably all deaf. But I'd take a breath and then make a move, no matter what. The sunrise would catch me and draw me the world. And that would be the best reason of all to wake, the most reliable, with the rising of the morning sun lifting my soul to new heights. It was hard to have any excuse when the sunlight would creep in through my bedroom window as if it was a thief stealing the night, and rest upon me just for a few seconds. It was as if it were trying to say, 'I'll blind you, my beggar, if you don't get up.'

Maybe it's just me, but isn't that the best reason of all? Finding one's feet could be very challenging, even for me. One could easily end up collapsing onto the floor and not even having a leg to stand on. You know what I mean. We've all been there. But when I'm up then I'm up, and there's never any wasting time searching for clothes, nor putting them on just to take them off or even wasting time falling in love with myself. It was never a problem since I never take my clothes off in the first place. I sleep in them. It was just a thing, and there's a very good reason for that.

Like I said, I hated change. It's bad for business. It's all about the misery and having my own style. And, most importantly, I never knew when I'd get the call from The Almighty. I wanted to be ready. All they have to do was slip a pair of shoes on me that wouldn't kill anyone, and I'd be off, leaving behind only the bits and bobs that I tossed into the fire. Ashes to ashes and dust to dust. There'd be nothing left. I could always say, 'God bless the beggar life. It's all gone up in smoke. A happy ending, even for him.' That was a very good reason, I like to think, for going to bed with your clothes on. And between you and me, if you thought of a better one, please let me know.

Yes, I have to admit I hated change in my life. This world of mine was perfect to me. Just a very simple room that contained only two small beds. One was mine and the other was a spare as sometimes it can get quite sweaty and hot, and I'd jump to the other one to cool me down. Trust me, I made many trips some nights. Oh, I nearly forgot, there was also a chair that I've never sat on. It's all about trust. Would its legs give up on me and let me down? I couldn't help it; it's just one of those things. You might even say, 'That's a little bit over the top.' Well, it's like this. I was born with a great set of legs underneath me, not a chair, and those are the ones I trust. Tucked away under the table is an unused flower vase – a reminder that I've never had the gentle touch of a sweet-scented flower in my life. If I had, I could easily have ended up with three beds in my room, which would've been a tight squeeze even for me. But for now, the vase sits there quietly enjoying a simple life. And there was nothing wrong with that.

If there were too many distractions then it ended up interfering with my thinking, and I'd never get to sleep. I would end up slipping from bed to bed all night long in the dark since there were no light switches. It would be a complete waste of time as I would never be able to find a switch in the dark. And they were no use during the day. All I've ever needed was an oil lamp that I always kept by my side. It provided me light in a world of darkness. It always had that faint flickering light of magic to it, enough to calm even the most tormented of souls. People of the world of plenty had their lights on night and day, given half a chance, but in my world there'd be no choice but to live their lives in the shadow of my falling stars. I liked to think of it as the beggar's shadow. It must be hard for them not to know if it was night or day, but this was no concern to me. Oh, but I loved that blessed silence at night. As I lay in bed, I listened and searched the howling winds for all the great battles that would be taking place between our two worlds, fighting for the greatest prize of all — the last flicker of light from my world.

Then, I hid underneath the silent covers of darkness. Yes, I'd be glad to stay in bed and listen to those voices from the past. They'd call me into the night, sharing with me their darkest secrets just to be saved in the nick of time by my flickering oil lamp. This would silence them and frighten them away, making me smile and say to myself, 'How lucky I am, even in darkness? There's always a small glimmer of hope even for a beggar such as I.'

I greeted most mornings with a crashing sound of sticks within a small opening in the corner of the room - a fireplace. The crows would spend most of the morning collecting twigs and trying to make their nests on top of the chimney pot, but it was all in vain. They could never get a grip on the biggest house. God bless them; they loved the high life. The higher, the better, as if they were in high order.

I removed the chimney cover in silence and stole from them their pile of twigs that would spill out onto the floor and clatter at my feet. The crows always gave me a steady supply of sticks for the fire. They were hard workers, those crows. There was no let-up from that crow family. It was only right that we lived in such heights. They tended to gather here, having a ruthless, snapping, picking aspect about them, just like myself. Well, what I'm trying to say is, if you didn't keep an eye on them then they'd pluck the eye right out of your head, and that would be the last you'd see of it.

So there you have it, never forgetting to put the cover back in its place and block such an opening. I could find myself with some company, as one of them could decide to come down the chimney and find out the great mystery of the missing twigs. Then they'd have something to flap about.

On the other side of the room, a wardrobe was resting quietly against the wall. Its entire life it always kept itself open as if to say, 'See? Everything is up for grabs.' Yes, it seems quite happy and content with its resting place, and that's where it's going to stay. There were two doors. One had a mirror on it that always reflected a perfect picture just for me. It was love at first sight every morning as I looked back at me, even though I never had time for such a thing. I'd even close my eyes and hide from such beauty. Then out of nowhere, it would catch my eye and wink at me as if to tell me, 'Who do you love, beggar of Blackthorn Hill?' Having a quick look around as if to see who it was talking to, I always returned to such beauty with a point of my finger at myself, and no matter how hard I tried, I could never escape from the perfect picture of beauty. Never wanting, or even asking me for anything in return, it's a perfect reflection of who I am that costs nothing. Yes, I could ask it anything, no matter what, and it would tell me everything I wanted to hear. Oh, such loyalty – just between ourselves. But it always ended up giving me a smile, as if to say, "You're looking good, my friend, and don't you worry; your secrets are safe with me." Yes, I see it again – a perfect picture of beauty as I look away, feeling a shame of being in the company of such greatness.

And if I had time, I would look to the other door of the wardrobe, where there was a slight crack, a hidden side where even those voices within would have their say and show me no mercy. They would tell me how they lurk in such a crack with a hidden greed. Please release me; always give me a picture of this real world they live in. But it didn't matter to me which side was looking out, as it's nothing without my reflection. To be fair, most of the time, it was always so kind and beautiful to me.

Even so, I'd have to listen to those internal voices. It was who I am. When I'd speak to them, my missing tooth would always spoil the view with a little pocket of darkness in my mouth. Yes, that crack in the mirror would never come to my rescue and save the morning images. Oh, the voices within told me not to worry about it. 'Beauty is only in the eyes of the beholder,' they said, 'And is nothing more than a fading weakness over time.' For instance, I was grand and blessed with having a good head of hair that was always holding its ground. But there was no taming it. It could swing from left to right, whatever way the wind was blowing, never losing its shape despite all the spit from my mother's mouth that landed on it when I was a young lad trying to tame it or even change its direction, but it was all in vain. It was too strong, even for the sternest hand. I just had to live with it, but I always tried to keep it out of sight, out of mind with my hat that covered my ears. And why not cover my ears? Half of everything I heard was rubbish anyway. So I'd tilt it forward, resting it against my nose. Well, it was grand. Like I said, I'm one of a kind, and if we were all the same, wouldn't life be boring? Never mind, there's no point talking about things we can't change.

But the most important thing that distinguished me and made me a great beggar was my nose. It had a slight tilt to one side. Not too sure which side, as this all depends on which eye was closed or which was opened when looking at it. Well, I like to think my strength is my beggar's nose because it never stops working. Maybe it was a true reflection of who I really am in this world of years.

Yes, the wardrobe had a mind of its own and couldn't be trusted, as life itself had given it a little bitterness within its depths. It never had colour, only those shadows of darkness always lying in wait for me. Maybe that was why it never showed me any mercy in the dead of night, as its doors would open with a little help from a nearby creaking, sagging floorboard when I'd step on it.

But most of the time, I felt like everybody else. I wouldn't change a thing no matter what. I always tried to find the best side of that reflection to keep me on my toes. But when I was up, I was up. Leaving my bed was a simple affair. There was never any pillow talk. It was just me, and all I had to do was drop my feet onto the stone-cold floor.

Oh yes, a chilling stiffness would shiver me up into a proper position. You could only get that in such a place as Blackthorn Hill. I would stand, snapping my braces against my chest, raising my shoulders high, lifting the legs of my pants over my ankles, and wiggling my toes just to say, 'Hello, boys. Would you like a set of matching socks? With or without holes? The choice is yours.' I could never find a perfect, matching pair of socks.

Or maybe that was simply a consequence of being colour-blind. Such is life. There's a reason for everything. But it was the fire that would be calling me, as its dying flame would whistle, 'Come on, beggar, it's breakfast time.' It never had any patience until it had its fill of fuel, a bit like myself. I'd fill it up with whatever was within reach from your world. Stand back. Wait and see what value your world had when it came to my hungry fire.

A light tangle of misty smoke would slowly rise before me and disappear up and away into the morning sky. Then, it would burst into flames with a sense of excitement as if to say, 'You saved my life, beggar. Now, give me more of this worthless rubbish from a world that has gone mad.' Yes, we'd be off to a fiery start. I'd spit into my hands and crash them together. Yes, I'm ready for a feast fit for a king. I would boil a pot of potatoes from the night before that had turned into a sticky, mossy paste known to me as pandy.

There was never any shortage of these potatoes; they grew wild in these parts. But me, I couldn't live without them. They were a delightful, simple pleasure. Even watching them boil over the flames of your world and turn everything that you hold dearly into a pile of worthless ash. Oh, how your worldly possessions mean nothing to me. I scooped my pandy and ate my fill of my pride and joy.

Chapter 7

Beggars Bowl

My wooden, beggar's bowl is simple. It has a crack on its side that catches everyone's gaze. It once belonged to a family of wealth and happiness, but over the years it lost its pride of place, so to speak, and was given to me. Yet everyone who passes stares at it with envy when they notice the joy it has provided me. There it sits, right by my side, as a reminder of a richer life. We enjoy each other's company. Its hidden treasures have made me king. I stand tall between these two great pillars of limestone with their firm grip upon the front door and guard this world of mine. Not even fear could make my door bow to the mighty westerly winds. It protects this house of mine; even I find it stern to the touch.

We have foraged a ruthless friendship of loyalty over the years, an unbreakable bond that make me trust it to do its job and protect all that I hold dear. That's all I've ever asked. Honestly, one of us couldn't live without the other. This beggar's house and I have a perfect relationship. Its walls are covered with a whitewash inside and out as if they were the scales of an old dragon that has turned grey but still retains the limey strength that signals it would kill whatever dared to invade its home. A bit like me, it never shows any mercy when it comes to this world.

The house's rafters are made from black oak. Time has made them harder than steel, bound and steepled together like the ribs of a great whale. The spiders have made their home here, their dusty webs dangling in the light and creating dazzling designs of splendour even master weavers would be envious of. Yet, the webs seal a ten-life sentence for whoever gets caught in them.

Between these two pillars of limestone is my home sweet home. We are of one kind. Nothing matters to us except what lies behind this door. Yes, it's the beggar's world that gives me my lifeblood. It runs through my veins like a natural spring bleeding from Mother Earth. It's who I am; I can't help it. I feel a sense of excitement overwhelming me as if it's a weakness when I stand in front of this solid oak door. The only release I get is to lay my hand upon its heavy bolt and slide it across.

Out of the darkness of that empty space, a gentle breeze slips under the door like a kiss of kindness. It brushes across my toes as a welcome to me. Only then do I capture that special moment. There's no guarantee in life that I might ever feel such a sensation again. I peek out and look down, checking to see if the coast is clear from unwanted visitors wanting to greet me and steal my magic all for themselves. After all, every king has an enemy. Only by following the set rules am I safe.

I like to think of these rules as a line that should never be crossed, no matter what. No one is above the laws of Mother Nature. Even something as small as a frog greeting me, trying to enter the house, would bring a lot of bad luck to me. Nothing would go right. Yes, we have our customs. They were handed down to me from our forefathers, and I love them. Something as simple as an irritated nose meant I was the topic of conversation. When struck by bad fortune, a simple task like putting on an item of clothing backwards would change it for the better. Or, flipping a coin into the air for fate to lead the way with heads or tails when standing at the crossroads of life. And if you were unsure about such rules, they could all be undone simply by throwing a pinch of salt over your left shoulder. No matter what one believed about such customs, they always brought a smile to onlookers. Performing them is just part of who I am. These acts made me the centre of attention, yes, but also ensured my path was safe. This place is the centre of my universe, as I said, and is known to all as Blackthorn Hill. I have lived my whole life in the shadow of this place. It got its name from the blackthorn bushes, but always had an unpredictable kindness to me despite the threat of the thorns. The bushes tilt their heads in harmony with the strong winds as if they were waving to me.

I loved this place; it was home. I could see myself in every twist and turn. Yes, we were one and needed no one else. Nothing mattered to us except the voices within telling me everything my heart desired. Mother Nature always held me by the hand, bringing me wherever was within her almighty breath and glance. I watched the twirling smoke stretch up into the morning sky and be blown away, showing me the chosen path. Oh, Mother Nature's great hand was always willing to help me along the way.

Whoever dared to challenge her or even face her down would be met with those hands of hers. Such a wilderness from her was beyond belief. Even for someone like me. And as I said, change was in the air, because these laws of nature were going to take their rightful place and rest upon my shoulders. But for now, this place of mine told me everything like it was an all-consuming first love. Trust me when I tell you, only a beggar such as I could live in such a place with this kind of love – we belonged to together. There was never anyone else. We often shared a weird kind of smile, especially when I spied seeds of wandering, lazy eyes as they tried to challenge us with their bright lights for a better life for everyone without a single concern for her, not even considering that our fate depends on which way her wind blows. It was up to me. 'Yes,' I shouted, my sharp beggar's voice echoing. 'What's this place to you? How dare you challenge my hill of blackthorn? She's mine. We are one in body and soul.' I never let myself forget else her mighty breath would strike me upon my face.

Oh, there was nothing gentle about her; even the oak trees bowed to her. Oh, she knew I was the last of my kind who had the strength to love her for who she was. Many times, I heard her search for me with a howling cry, 'Where are you, my beggar?' There was no escape from her. All I could do was close my eyes and wait for her gentle breeze to rest upon my cheeks and kiss me on my lips, letting me know that she would search for me even in death. What could I say? It was love. That simple pleasure lifted my spirit, but it was short lived. Love alone waits for no man, not even the beggar of Blackthorn Hill.

The strong scent of virgin white roses challenged me. They had a mind of their own, their whistling carried to me on the wind from all directions, saying, 'Let's see what the beggar's love is made of, and if he deserves such loyalty to what we hold dear.' Only then would I fight them with my bare hands – with everything I had. There was no holding back as I surrendered and raised my hands over their heads and squeeze my lifeblood upon them, turning the roses a fiery red. Surely, this blood of mine would quench their thirst for love and make us one of a kind. Hopefully, this alone would silence them. Yes, all we had was each other. That was all I ever wanted in my life. If you decide to climb my hill of the blackthorn, there would be nothing waiting except a path of pain and misery and a sharp beggar's tongue. Having no one to blame but yourself since you might never see another day. This hill of blackthorn would back me up, no matter what was said.

Yes, I knew every path, pebble, and hidden stone that lay beneath my feet. I gazed upon Mother Nature's charming beauty during every sunrise and sunset. This was all I ever wanted in life, just like the people before me. I'm sure they died happy knowing I was here. That she wasn't alone and was in safe hands. This made me bow my head in sadness when I saw her silent tears resting on the heathers, knowing the others before me were long gone. 'Yes,' I said to her, 'I am the last of my kind.' All I could ever do was talk to her and give her the comfort that I would never let her go without a fight. As I looked to the world of plenty with its empty promises, it would shout even louder, 'Stay away!', because there was no place here to hide. The hill of blackthorn would capture your soul and strip it clean of what you held dear, leaving nothing but wasted dreams shredded upon the blackthorn bushes. I pluck them and let them blow in the wind, hoping they found their rightful owners. This was no place for such dreams, as the swirling wind would change my direction and bring me within her hand of strength. 'Come on, beggar,' she would say. 'I have a very special place for you,' and she would never let me down with such hidden beauty. It always brought me to tears of joy. She could easily turn her seasons to sorrow and sadness with her cruel hand of nature, easily shove me over cliff's edge to a place where there would be no return, not even for a beggar.

Well, it always depended on which way her wind would be blowing. She could also give me the power for whatever my heart desired – even to make time itself stand still for an eternity. All I had to do was ask. She's the only one who ever understood me and who I really am. We'd been together since I took my first breath of her mighty winds and was blessed when her waters poured over my head, and I drank from her spring that flowed from deep within her heart. Nothing would ever separate us, not even death itself. Yes, I could safely say we enjoy each other's company even in the darkest of winter nights. I could hear her taunting whispers telling me tales about the souls she captured from this world and took to the next, leaving nothing but helpless screams that terrified everyone. Even I would shiver, seeing as I was just a humble beggar. Yes, I am the last of my kind, despite her dizzy heights getting a little higher with every passing year.

I'd stop and say to her, 'I'm just a beggar that time has forgotten. Please wait for me so I can catch my breath.' That was all I needed to give me the strength to stand and gaze upon her beauty, watching her chase the darkness away as it tried to cross the Valley of the White Horse. They never escaped her blinding sun. I, the beggar of Blackthorn Hill, would sit on a great slab of stone and watch another world come to life spurred on by its hunger for all things great. It would scatter all of these great things in all directions, leaving nothing but wandering trails of smoke in the sky that searched for their lost owners. Many times I saw them question themselves, asking the silence, 'How could a beggar have such happiness in his life and never ask for anything, even when he is in our world of plenty?' Well, it doesn't matter; it's grand.

I would only ever ask her to sing me a sweet lullaby as I would pick a piece of wild grass and place it between my thumbs. Then, I'd blow alongside the freshness of her lungs as she sang a melody with such seasonal splendour. It would flow through the valleys, capturing even the wildest of hearts. There was no escape as the pheasants would delightfully take flight and land again, resting their heads with a sense of pride as they answered her call. As I listened to the morning chatter, their voices would rise with the morning sun before being silenced by the cuckoo, as if to say, 'Get into tune.' Nothing mattered up here except life and the great will to live it just for one day.

I opened my coat and stretched my hands into the air so they flapped like a great set of wings capturing her almighty strength, lifting me off my feet as if I were floating in mid-air. But I knew my time enjoying this sense of freedom would be short-lived. My calling would eventually arrive, telling me, 'Home is where the heart is,' and only then would I take my assigned path and stop at the blue pool that gives this hill of the blackthorn its lifeblood and quenches its thirst. Its waters were crystal clear and would only come to stillness when it chatted with me. It was quite willing to share its wealth of pure honesty to quench my thirst for great knowledge. It would show me all the wrinkled paths that I could have collected over the years. But I'd close my eyes and hide within a world of darkness for a while, always finding the inner strength to reach out and strike its stillness. I hoped all would be carried away within its ripples of time and let me know I was as much a part of her as she is of me. I would never let her go.

I just can't help it; it's who I am – the beggar of Blackthorn Hill. But I really must apologise to you, as sometimes I got caught up in my own world and forgot who I really am. I just couldn't help it. By some chance, if you were looking for me, which is very unlikely, you'd find me in the place I love the most – among the blackthorn bushes on the side of my hill. We always shared the same kind of stubbornness; we wanted everything our way, and certainly refused give an inch. It was just one of those places where you would have to give it your all and was especially trying when I had to cut branches from the white roses for the winter fire as if it was as simple as giving them a haircut. And there was nothing wrong with that. But most of the time, I felt a sense of anger, knowing I wasn't going to have everything my way. Especially when the branches would be waving a crown of thorns over my head.

Given half the chance, they would be quite willing to place it upon me. Then I'd know the meaning of real pain. But I am a beggar and would know when to take a step back before all would come crashing down and crumble at my feet. Then I'd say to myself, 'That was a good one. It had in a kind of fighting spirit to the end.'

'Oh yes,' I would say, 'You remind me of myself,' and never forgetting how the hidden strength of Mother Nature could sneak up behind me and easily steal my prize right underneath my nose, sending it tumbling down the side of the cliff and being the last I see of it. I would be left there with nothing, asking myself, 'How did this happen to someone like me?'

'Yes,' I'd say to Mother Nature, 'You got me. I never saw you coming. What could I do except look at my hands? Maybe they are losing their grip.' The minute she hit the ground, I'd grab on for dear life. No time for thinking. Has she given up the fight or is she lying low underneath the soft blanket of moss, waiting to give me a proud thorn into my finger to share her dying pain with me? Oh, such pain, I would never forget it and would stay with me for most of the day as a reminder to me and she'd say, 'Listen, beggar, this fight isn't over until I've gone up in smoke.'

Indeed, this hill of blackthorn was certainly not for the faint-hearted. As many times as I got prodded by them, I would bite them from my finger, spit them onto the ground, and stomp on them. Yes, I would. I would stomp them right into the rich soil. 'Well,' I would say to them, 'Someday, you'll make a fine blackthorn bush. After all, was your first drink not the beggar's blood? That would certainly give you the strength you need to live among us on Blackthorn Hill.' Only then did I hear a church bell. Its high tone would catch my ear. It only ever meant one thing to me - the odd neighbour would soon appear out of nowhere. He would be in a hurry to answer its call of forgiveness, hopefully making his soul a little lighter and giving his spirit a helping hand along the way.

When he saw me, he'd shout, 'God bless the good work, beggar,' just to let me know his mind and soul were on a similar journey of forgiveness. Despite him living within my shadow, I'd turn my head with such a fright when he called to me. Even though his journey had always been like the Stations of the Cross – having a story of twists and turns to tell about this beggar of Blackthorn Hill. As I looked to the heavens and muttered a few silent words, 'Nobody's closer to you than me when I claim my hill.' I wondered if there was anyone out there brave enough to stand by my side and give me a helping hand to fight for my hill of blackthorn? No, it wasn't looking good. It was just me and the voices within, straightening up at the clicking sound coming from my back that kept me company.

There was no need to save my soul; it had been lost in this world of pain and madness of mine. I smiled to the heavens and gave it a wink, as if to say, 'I wouldn't have it any other way.' Yes, there was always a reason for everything in my world. Maybe they were all afraid of my hill, the blackthorn, and it was decided a very long time ago that there was never any plan for this beggar. But for now, well, I didn't care. Beauty was in the eyes of the beholder, and I liked what I saw. Why not? It was me, and what you saw was what you got. And that was what happened. It was all about how you lived in this world of mine. Like I said, I never had a choice. I was born into it. There was plenty of pain in here to last me a lifetime, spotting a few more souls rushing along, hoping to make it before that final strike. But don't worry about it. The most important thing was to keep a watchful eye on my blackthorn bush that had fallen from grace, as this was the only real thing in my world and all I ever needed. I turn my back to all in that world of plenty that had gone soft. They have too much time on their hands, and they have so much of it. I hear them say they would take a day off to do nothing. That makes no sense to me. Well, that's one thing I can say – I never had a day where I had nothing to do. Maybe in a way, they are lost souls searching for a happy ending.

My father always said, 'Show me your hands and I will tell you who you are.' Those were wise words from a very wise man. I often said to myself, 'There's nothing wrong with someone shouting to me, "How's the beggar of Blackthorn Hill?"' I love to hear such a calling. It separated me from everyone else. I like to think it was nice to be different. If we were all the same, what type of world would we live in?' To be fair, that's who I am, and it made me king of my world. Destiny had arrived in all its glory, and there was no escape. It sent a shiver across my back. I couldn't shake it. Not even with my back to the fire. It made me nervous, to be honest with you. I worried there was a hidden draught in the house, and it might be trying to escape.

I looked outside just to check the weather. Nothing. Not even a nip in the air. Quite calm. But there it was again, another shiver running across my back and onto my shoulders. There was no mistaking it; I was being watched. Call it my beggar's instinct. I felt it in my bones. There was a smell in the air. Not a strong smell like you'd get from roadkill. No, nothing like that. The smell of incense. Stroking my beard is just one of those things I do when I'm very nervous.

I noticed the autumn leaves had shifted to one side as if clearing a path leading to my front door. At that very moment, I was startled by the strike of a loud bang coming from behind me. The old clock started striking upon the hour as its pendulum swung with a sense of urgency – the loss of time. Yes, it struck dead on one with an almighty bang. I felt its echo ripple right through me and further up in the valley, startling thousands of starlings into flight. They were in the thousands, blackening out the sky as they twisted and turned like flying was a new sense of freedom for them. I'd never seen such a display. Now, what was all that about? There was nothing in my beggar's rule book about starlings taking flight and working together as one. No, it was everyone for themself in this world of mine.

And what of the clock? Surrendering that moment in time it had enjoyed as long as I can remember. The sky had cleared of starlings, gone as quickly as they had taken flight as if the heavens had opened and swallowed them. And that wasn't the only thing that was disappearing. My hill of blackthorn was beginning to be covered by a stark white blanket of snow right before my eyes. It was going to be an early winter, which was unusual. Simply, I hated surprises – I never see them coming. But deep down, I knew things weren't right; change was in the air. I could smell it as the snow started to pile up into drifts, blocking all paths connecting my world to yours.

Nothing was left except a strong, cutting breeze. My world was gone. In its place was this white wonderland, freezing me within its tight grip. There was nothing wrong with that. So, sit with me and gaze upon the flames of plenty. Share with the past, the present, or even the future, whatever your heart desires. But destiny will straighten the beggar's door tonight and we'll decide the future for all. But for now, while we wait for such a calling, it's the glimmer of the past that I wanted to share with you. One that eroded over time, leaving nothing but blinding dust.

I had a younger sister and an older brother. He was nothing like me; he could put his ear to Blackthorn Hill, hear its haunting sounds, and whistle them into the wind. Even to this day, I heard them calling to me with an irresistible, tormenting plea for such a soul. Many times, I'd fall to my knees and put my ear to the ground but could never find such a calling of that watchful eye over us. My sister always had a great sense of joy, living a life of hope for the good of all mankind. It didn't matter if it was night or day to her since she couldn't sleep without that great sense of colour, blinding everything before and after her.

She was gifted with the voice of an angel and would sing at the cliff edge as everyone gazed upon her beauty to what type of soul would be enjoying such a dangerous perch. One night, she fell silent, her voice gone with the wind, and she took with her that great splash of splendour. But I always smiled and thought of her when I saw a rainbow. After she vanished, I searched for her high and low; it was in vain. And if I asked about her, I was told she's beneath us now and to never speak of her again. My brother's time soon came and went. So he left, too, disappeared into a cloud of dust of bright lights. To this day, when I see such a cloud of dust rise before me, I reach out to greet it, hoping that when it clears, he'd be standing there.

'Yes,' I said to you, 'I am the beggar of Blackthorn Hill, sitting here by the fire with these memories from the past that never leave my side. It's like they were taunting me.' I looked at my hands with their silent strength. If only my hand could capture them and bring them home. I heard those voices within my head telling me I would never find strength like the fear of losing your one true love, Blackthorn Hill. There would be nothing left. Only a shadow of darkness – of dead silence.

'Yes,' I said to you, 'Goodnight. It's time for you to go.' Even though I had enough and only wanted to sleep underneath this great blanket of snow, I couldn't. With a blinding flash of light, it was as if I was frozen in time and stiff as a poker, all except for my beggar's eye. It started to search the house before getting snared on a spider's web as if I was the catch of the day. There he sat, the larger of the two spiders. Buttons, that's what I called him. Because he liked to wrap and roll his catch. He started to shuffle and was on the move – he was never in a hurry. Nice and easy, always enjoying his victim's last second of time. And there he was, dangling inches from my eye. With one snap from his mighty claws, I'd be gone and never to be seen again. I thought, 'How can I live without a gift that kept me on my toes and never let me rest?' We gazed into each other's eyes with nothing but a sense of trust between us. Yes, I could see his world glittering. He had such freedom to enjoy the present, to live his life as if it were the last day for all living things. Capturing a moment of happiness, bringing a tear of shame to me for never knowing such a pleasure.

'Oh,' the voices within said, 'Fear, my beggar, is the only real thing in this world of ours. Rise from the occasion, my beggar, from such paralyzing stillness. Imagine. Such a presence. Crush him if that's what your heart desires. Such loyalty is always rewarded without judgment. It's fear that has kept us united in this world of ours. Are you not the beggar of Blackthorn Hill? The master of all? Even the wise old oak trees have bowed to you. Such a fear I speak of since a single strike from your mighty hand would send everything crashing down, turning everything into to a pile of ash. Fear is the lifeblood that flows through our veins.'

Without you, I am nothing. The door shook with terror, startling the spider and sending him back up into the safety of his web. There it was again – a silent strike that I could only hear. Maybe it was the noises of the night. This was what happened when I stayed up all night with the voices within. No, it definitely wasn't them; they were with me. Yes, something was at the door. I could hear my heart beating as if it was telling me, 'Beware! We've never heard such a sound before.' Maybe it was the snow sliding from the corrugated iron roof and crashing to the ground. Yes. That made me relax with a sense of relief. What a great house this was. Even when the heavens open, it showed me her strength and love for me. Not even the voices could argue with that. A happy ending for all.

But then I heard a scratching sound. Or was it a gentle knock? Whatever it was, it had arrived at my front door. It certainly wasn't the sound of crashing snow. Maybe it was the sound of the night in conflict. Even though I knew it wasn't, I had to see it so I could enjoy that brief second of happiness of knowing what it was. But deep down, the beggar in me was warning that what waited beyond the door would change my life forever. There would be no way out, not even for this beggar. Even so, I'd have to hold my ground. Or maybe the knock upon the door carried bit of respectability. If it were a wild animal, there would be no knocking; they would want to tear it down. Oh, where are the voices within when I needed them? They had left me for the hills, leaving me to speak from a further point of view. Whatever it was could only stand outside for so long in this freezing snow. Surely it would lose its fiery spark. With such a chill, another knock arrived upon my door. This time it carried with it an understanding of who it was, like whatever it was finally realised they were in my world now. It was after cooling their heels. Oh, the voices in my head were back now. 'Beggar,' they said, 'Your time is right. Reach for your blackthorn stick and open the door. We'll take it from there.'

The stick had been in the family for years. My father used to let me hold it with a sense of pride and told me the story of how we came to be, just like he was told by his father. There had been a great fire on the hill of blackthorn, and all was destroyed except for one blackthorn bush at the top of the hill. The toughest, meanest, and ugliest. Not even the flames of Hell could destroy it. A branch that bush was cut and used to propagate the ruined land and brought the hill back to life. And now it's mine. I keep it by my side as if a judge and journey for all. I squeezed it within my hand this night, giving me the support I need like a true friend, having a crown upon it that would split these two worlds of ours in half. Its blackness would dim the lights of all who stood before it. It struck fear in all that stood against it.

The voices within said, 'Strike, my beggar. On this very night with all the power of Blackthorn Hill within. Let it land right between their eyes. Yes, dim their lights. Leave nothing but darkness.'

'Oh,' the voices said, 'We're ready, beggar. Open the door now, beggar.' Squeezing the blackthorn stick in my left hand, I raised it over my head. Yes, that was my most reliable hand. I had depended on it to dish out pain many times. The right hand had softened over the years, so the right hand got the easy job. All it had to do was slide the bolt across, nice and easy, and get out of the way of my left hand.

Quick as I could, I prepared to strike – the blackthorn stick was going to do all the talking. I was going to solve all my problems tonight with a single mighty swing. Something or someone was going to end up with their lights out – a starry night, in beggar's language, or a very good night's sleep. I clenched my teeth and rested my lazy eye while I sharpened my beggar's eye. I was ready. I slid the bolt across and quickly shuffled my right hand behind my back – job done, nice and safe. My left hand was poised to strike no matter what. I wouldn't question my determination to get the job done as if I had been tossed a few words of encouragement to say I was lucky to have you by my side and if you couldn't take them out, you'd definitely take them down. It was as simple as that. The door started to open; I was ready. I let out a roar. The black stick came crashing down and struck the ground.

To my surprise, I found myself covered in snow. I'd sent it flying in all directions with such force that I made it splash. I realized the door had opened from the weight of the snow. I missed and feared that splash of snow would be the very last sound I heard before death. Or was it the sound of death itself? The death of a beggar like me, falling from grace while covered in snow. I took a step back and kept my beggar's eye focused on the door, knowing it was too late to close it. I was frozen in fear, not even blinking, since what was waiting for me might be an eternity of darkness. Thought, I still had enough time for one more strike. 'Oh,' the voices within said, 'Get a grip. You are the beggar of Blackthorn Hill and will never lay down in the snow to die like a wild animal. When they enter the house of the beggar of Blackthorn Hill, they will bow to you from fear of the blackthorn stick.'

All that separated me from my fate this night was a large pile of snow that covered my feet, a shivering chill right through me. But it had a calming effect as if everything was peaceful in the beggar's house this night. I could feel the power of my left hand losing its grip, lifeless, falling to my side and dropping the blackthorn stick. My power was gone. I was helpless, just like the snow that had fallen from the heavens. Its fate had already been decided. It was only a matter of time for me. But what appeared before me was no angel of death. It was a small, child-like figure. It kept its distance between us, saying, 'You have nothing to fear in the beggar's house this night.' I grabbed the oil lamp and cast a glimmer of light in the distance toward the stranger. A white mist started to rise before me, surrounding everything as my world started to fade. It was gone, taken from me like it never existed.

I heard a soft voice whisper, 'You are known to me, the beggar boy.' I raised the lamp within to see a more clearly. I was greeted by crystal blue eyes that carried a joyful stillness within them, an internal happiness that was only known to me and contained all my dreams within their deep blue pool. But this stranger had a brightness within not just for me, but for all. 'Yes,' I said, 'I'm - ' And with that, I closed my eyes as my whole life flashed before me. When I opened them, tears of joy wet my face as if the spirit of Blackthorn Hill was with me.

I imagined a celebration of my life in this world that gave me everything my heart desired. The last person to call me the beggar boy had departed many years ago and never returned. But what stood before me was no child. 'Yes,' I said, 'I was known as the beggar boy, but now I'm just the beggar.' The stranger was wrapped in a shawl that glittered like it was embedded with flawless diamonds. The scent of the wilderness, just out of reach, drifted around them. Even though she came in the dark of the night, there was a glimmer of light within her. After I closed the door, I turned around and realised she had made her way over to the windowsill. She stared at an old photo of my family, but something had changed about this gathering. The hill of blackthorn stood firm as if it had our back. She looked at me and said, 'Indeed, this is the biggest house.' She turned her head towards me. 'Don't you know me? I watched over you every day, my beggar boy.'

'I live alone. I've never seen you before. Maybe it's the light from the oil lamp; it can play tricks. Maybe it's not strong enough. Sit by the fire.' She did as I directed.

I captured her face as it appeared to me; yes, she was of small build but had a calmness about her, a silence. It was her strength, just like my tree of knowledge. Even though she was delicate as its leaves, I knew deep down inside she was here for a reason. Changes were in the air that night. Things would never be the same again. I said, 'I'm just a beggar who lives his life in a forgotten world of shadow and darkness where time stands still.' She unwrapped her shawl, releasing her hair. It was so dark it seemed to hold the night as it flowed over her shoulders. Her skin was pale but held a good grip of youthfulness. Her clothes were easy on the eye. The colours were so strong and fresh that it was as if they were all seasons wrapped in one. I noticed she was not alone and carried a developing life within her. I said, 'You're going to be a mother.'

'Yes,' she said, 'It's the greatest gift of all.' She smiled. At that very moment, I remembered such a smile that brought lightness even in the deepest darkness. That smile belonged to my sister, lost in this world just like me. She had given me everything my heart desired and never asked for anything in return. 'Yes,' she said, 'But tonight, I ask of one act of kindness from you, the beggar of Blackthorn Hill. Reach into the darkness for what lies before you tonight, in the world of plenty. This will unite the past, present, and future of both our world and theirs. This alone will allow us to live freely with a sense of loyalty to you, my beggar. Even nations will bow their heads in shame for never knowing such happiness. Only you, the beggar of Blackthorn Hill, have such inner strength. Only if your heart desires will everything fall silent. Even the voices within.'

'How can this be? I'm just a beggar.'

'This world of mine only takes pity upon me, while another doesn't even see me. All I can do is hide within their shadows.'

'This is true, my beggar. Even so, our fate lies before you this night.'

The night seemed broken by the howling wind, wanting to have its say.

'Oh,' the voices within said, 'Who has stood by your side? Don't listen to her, beggar, we've got your back. Look away from her; you can't trust her. Gifting you such power that's there for the taking if your heart desires it is nothing more than an illusion – a weakness – to be preyed upon by everyone. What's in it for you? Nothing. You said it yourself many times. The echoes have filled this valley many times for all to hear. Yes. What's in it for you? Nothing.

'Reaching out, the world of plenty has nothing we want. Its fear has given you strength, my beggar, to live in the place we call Blackthorn Hill. Let them live their lives within our shadows. Don't trust her; she's weak. Maybe she's trying to steal your soul from your one true love, Blackthorn Hill. That's it, beggar. How can the fate of all be your responsibility on this night? It's a trick. You're the beggar of Blackthorn Hill. We are the voices within. Remember those wise words that have made you king and have given you the strength to live your life without shame. And the fate of all will lie before you this night. Fear, my beggar. If only you could ask your dear old friend, the witch, it's that world of plenty that gave her the arch in her back. She's seen enough to last a lifetime.'

The voices within continued, 'We'll never let you go. Unite us with this world of plenty she speaks of tonight. They carry a virus of greed within. All that's left for them is to fall in love with themselves. Yes, their fate may lie before you tonight. It's all about trust. We are the voices within, and the only real thing right now is your blackthorn stick. Strike them down in their hour of weakness.'

As the darkness of such a thought closed in around me, we hardly spoke a word of such a thing. The howling winds battled the night as if the fate of all was going to be decided before dawn.

As the fire continued to consume and burn through its life, the voices within yelled, 'The night is ours, as fate decrees.' The fire lost its spark. Even the shadows of the house had disappeared into encroaching darkness, calling it a night. I looked at her and pointed to Blackthorn Hill; maybe it had been decided a long time ago this was going to be our final resting place. I'm just a humble beggar. I handed her a patchwork quilt that had such splendid colours on it, hoping this would give her comfort during the night. It was as if she would be sleeping underneath a rainbow. Surely, this would make her smile, knowing that each patch of colour came from a place of goodwill and carried a blessing within. It might bring her the happiness she had been searching for. As the house fell silent and the wind calmed, I could feel a sense of excitement in the night that not everything was lost. There was still time. I could hear my heartbeat as if it was a clock on the wall that was counting down the minutes. I felt I was waiting for the mighty strike of a great cry, and suddenly there it was. I jumped to my feet, and lo and behold, looking down, my feet had landed right into my shoes. I didn't even have to think about it. A cry called to me, 'Beggar, the hour of our new life is nearly upon us. This gift of life I carry will wait no longer.'

I squeezed my eyes tight, hoping it was just a dream. That when I opened them, there a happy ending for all.

Unfortunately, everything was the same. I was never any good under pressure. Didn't even have anywhere to go. I never had been since nobody wanted me in the first place. At that very second, a robin entered the house and landed on the table in front of me. It tilted his head in my favour as if telling me this mother and child were meant to be delivered into this world that I feared. But even so, maybe the child's destiny had already been decided. Maybe its heart would be pure and would always belong to Blackthorn Hill. I thought, 'No, this world of mine is no place for a newborn. The best I can do is bungle it all together and get them off the hill of blackthorn as quickly as possible.'

'Oh,' the voices within said, 'At last, the beggar has a plan. We love it. Out of sight, out of mind. Two's company, but three's a crowd. There's nothing in this for you, my beggar. Remember, everyone has a price. Take her to the large town, beggar. There's a building there that has lights on all the time. It's perfect for the mother-to-be, and this newborn doesn't even care if it's night or day. It's all about timing with them. Anyway, this could be what she was asking of you. Let's go, beggar. It's a small price to pay for our own happiness. They'll look after her and this newborn. They have a great life amongst their own. Let's go; it shouldn't take long. She's travelling light; she has nothing with her.'

'Yes,' I said to myself, 'I will hook up the trap to Wild Bill.'

Wild Bill was a stray donkey that had wandered onto Blackthorn Hill and never left. He enjoyed freedom as much as I did, and he sheltered against the house even in wintertime. He'd get us there, and so we were off. Even though he was small in size, he ploughed through the snow. He cocked his ears at me now and again as if to say, 'I know the meaning of bearing a cross upon my back for such a task like this.' But when all was said and done, it didn't matter to him. If there was twenty feet of snow in front of Wild Bill and he wanted to go straight, he'd plow right through. That's what I liked about Wild Bill. In a way, I saw a lot of myself in him. We were made for each other.

I spotted the neighbours' houses glittering with their fancy-coloured lights. The glow made it seem as if they were dancing in the snow. What's all that about? I hoped not to be spotted at this time of night. I'd be the talk of the land. They'd say, 'There's the beggar taking a ride on a donkey, pulling a cart with a mother-to-be.' Looking to the heavens, I thought, 'Imagine if the two of us were found frozen to death.' Oh, the thought of that alone could kill someone. What would they say about me at my funeral? 'We always knew the hill would kill him. Where was he going with a pregnant woman?'

That alone brought a tear to my eye as I cast my other eye up to the heavens, thinking, 'I'm not ready to die like this. I want to die on Blackthorn Hill with my Blackthorn stick by my side, not a pregnant woman.' I crossed my eyes to look at a droplet of water that had frozen and turned to crystal. I watched it turn frosty white.

If that wasn't bad enough, it started to tickle my nose. There was no way I was going to wipe my nose in front of a woman. That wasn't my style. Waste not, want not – that's me. Sniffing it up like I was having a quick lunch on the move was the true beggar style. Wiping my nose with a tissue or whatever was a sign of weakness in my profession. With a sharp sniffle I solved the problem – out of sight, out of mind. But what followed was excruciating pain as if a spear had pierced the back of my throat. I opened my mouth against such pain, and, with an almighty sneeze, everything went flying out my nose. It struck Wild Bill on the back with an almighty splat, giving him such a fright that he took off.

I'd never seen him move so fast. I held on for dear life. It was as if we were surging through the clouds of white, dusty, smoky snow. I couldn't see anything, and I didn't care. I knew there was only one direction for Wild Bill – straight. There was no stopping him. We passed a small child that was looking out a window and they waved at us. There was no stopping us. I looked for any signs that would tell me where we were or even where we were headed, but all I saw was a bad bend at the bottom of the hill. If that didn't kill us, we'd never survive the humpback bridge. It would surely send us flying in all directions. 'Yes,' I said to myself, 'Even for a beggar, I had a lot on my mind tonight. There was certainly no point in hoping for a happy ending.' I knew we were getting closer as I could hear the melting snow slush beneath us. Even Wild Bill had enough and was slowing down just in the nick of time.

When we came to a sudden stop, I said, 'Even if I was blinded by the snow, this street would be well known to me.' It was Angel Lane.

Chapter 8

Angel Lane

I didn't recognise it because of the beautiful angels suspended above me and showering me with love. I recognised it because of the back lane that ran parallel to the main streets. The splendour of streets such as these would blind you with its dazzling lights of beauty and empty promises of a great life. There was a price to be paid for everything, especially whatever your heart desired. I should know; nothing was for nothing in this world. Angel Lane seemed to offer a mother's love to everyone equally, gifting a new sense of freedom. Ye, it seemed at first glance to be a fair exchange of goods for such freedom. But with the passage of time, those empty promises amounted to nothing more than the haunting tears of shame that never let one rest and never knowing innocence as if one had been stolen from one's mother's arms. 'Yes,' I say to myself, 'Just empty promises for a better life; that's all they whisper of along Angel Lane.' But I managed to find a smile within for the greatest gift of all – hope. Even though I lived a life as a beggar and struggled amidst life's gutter, with the strength of time I could spot those ageing eyes; they always returned, searching Angel Lane for the great loss of all, never knowing a mother's love. I knew that look and would say to them, 'It's easier to carry the weight of forgiveness upon one's shoulders than a lifetime of shame.'

Oh, Wild Bill, why Angel Lane? I knew of this building with its condemning light as if it was judge and jury for whoever stood beneath it. Oh, the voices within argued, 'But to be fair, are you not a beggar of Blackthorn Hill? What's in it for you?'

'Nothing,' I admitted, 'Even guilt has only ever fallen upon deaf ears in Angel Lane. Guilt is nothing more than a great boulder that no one wants to carry. With the passage of time, it becomes nothing more than a pebble bearing the pride and joy of a mother's love as experienced by a newborn child.'

The voices within said, 'Such wisdom you have, beggar. Forget Angel Lane; it's not for you and your silent tears of shame. Listen to us; we've got your back. You are the last of our kind to speak these words of wisdom. Though, to be fair, are we not without shame? But such is life, as we have nothing to offer a world of plenty this night.' But Angel Lane was mute as if it was expecting us. Something was up; trust me. Even I found the streets quiet. Nothing was there but a streetlight holding its ground with a firm grip. It cast a shadow of doubt upon me. I figured that tonight the dagger of Blackthorn would stand in its shadow of shame, which as some would call the end of the line.

I tied Wild Bill to the streetlight as it flickered in the night; it was as if it was fidgeting, trying to make up its mind to glimmer with light or stay hidden in the dark. As I crossed the lane, I found myself standing in the shadowy door of empty promises just like those who came before me. 'It's the easy way out, beggar,' the voices within said, 'A quick fix. That's all we need this night, then everything will be back to normal. One act of kindness. Surely, this is what she spoke of tonight. As I looked into the light, I wondered if I was being blinded. Such a strong flickering light. What of all who have stood before me and their words of wisdom? Looking at my sister, I realised her faith rested in the hands of a beggar tonight. 'What should I do?' I wondered, looking around. Nothing, not even a whisper in response. It was as if the whole world was waiting to see what the beggar Blackthorn Hill was going to do. Well, most of the time, doing nothing was the best plan. Especially for me. Not tonight.

As I stood in the shadow of this door covered in a white blanket of snow, I admit it was quite pleasant to look at. But looks could be deceiving in a place like this. A black knocker in the shape of a lion's head rested against the door with a sense of pride and place; it seemed quite willing to feast on the touch of whoever dared answer its call. But I worried about what was hidden underneath this perfect picture of white snow as I raised my hand and brushed it off. After all, I am the beggar of Blackthorn Hill, and life taught me there was nothing to lose by taking one step back. Why not? It gave me a clear picture of what lied beneath. Now, what stood before me was a door of solid black oak. 'Yes,' I said to myself, 'This is a fitting challenge for such a beggar as I.'

I lean forward and with one sniff of my beggar nose to confirm that, yes, I know this door of black oak. I remember when it was a sapling planted by my father's hand. He stood over it, and I watched it grow in a place called Limestone Ridge, a barren and windswept cliffside. That place always carried a sense of grandeur for me. Only the strongest could thrive there. But I must say, it was a very fitting spot for such a tree until the day it lost its grip on life and fell from grace, leaving nothing but a cold chill in its place.

'So,' I thought, 'This is your final resting place, trapped among this arch of stone on Angel Lane. Quite happy to be the judge and jury for whoever stands before you.' It was as if there was nothing but a brief moment in time for me to rest my pan upon it. Yes, I could feel the door's bitterness for life. This place gave it nothing but twisted knots. It was a far cry from the sense of freedom it enjoyed at Limestone Ridge, and now its only friend in this world was the blinding light hanging over my head. Looking up, I knew there was no hiding place for whoever stood beneath it; their shadowed, haunting past never let them go. I have seen it myself, especially when they tried to hide themselves within such beauty.

The voices within told me to strike the door. That it was destiny. They said, 'You are our one true love. Strike the door, beggar. Fear nothing. Why should you? Are you not the chosen one? Strike it, my beggar; it's a small price to pay for such loyalty to us. Trust us, beggar. Think of the sense of freedom we have together. You can do it. Strike it for our world; there's nothing better than that.'

'Oh, voices in my head, how right you are,' I thought. 'Yes, I am the beggar of Blackthorn Hill. This has always been about me.'

The voices replied, 'You are our one true love and the last of your kind. Only you can rise to such an occasion.' And so I did, striking the door with the lion head and standing back. I listened to the resulting caw like crows summoning their master. I heard a clicking of a switch on the other side, sending a sliver of light underneath the door, followed by the gentle pat of soft shoes making their way to the door.

Suddenly, there was silence and the line of light seeping under the door was broken. There was someone here, now. I could tell the person on the other side of the door was slight, having a delicate build. They were certainly no match for the presence of a beggar like me. The silence was broken by a clanging sound of keys as they searched right one. 'Oh,' the voices within said, 'Tonight is your night, indeed. They are weak-minded, unsure of themselves, and untrustworthy. But that in itself is a weakness, beggar. If they were of strong mind, they would have been heavy-footed and would have a tight grip upon the night's keys. They certainly wouldn't need a light to show them the way. You're not going to be judged this night. Why would you? Aren't you just a beggar without shame? This has always been your hidden strength. Even this door of black oak has fallen from grace, and it had a good grip on life.'

Yes, it was all about first impressions in this world of plenty. Then, the moment of no return arrived with a clicking sound unlocking the door. As it opened, I kept my eyes on the ground and focused on a pile of snow. It didn't dare follow the line of the door. Maybe I couldn't cross unless invited. Or maybe the snow knew something that I didn't.

From the door appeared a pair of black shoes that had lost their shine were well-worn on the tip, which was a sign of a forgiving heart. But most noticeable of all was the set of loosely tied laces, which meant there would be no judgment tonight. Only a fair exchange of goods for my freedom. I glanced up; a slight woman dressed all in black stared straight at my face and put her hand up to her mouth as if she had swallowed something without chewing it. Or maybe it was being in the great presence of a beggar such as me tonight in this world of plenty. Behind her was a gathering.

I made to speak but was interrupted by a voice, 'Stand to one side; out of my way.'

Then, another voice asked, 'Who is it, and what do they want on a night like this?'

'It's a beggar. Have you ever seen one before?' She took her rightful place in front of everyone, standing before me with her hands folded across her chest. She seemed to me a tower of strength that had weathered many storms and came out the other side unscathed.

'Oh,' the voices said, 'Remember, beggar, it's your freedom we speak of tonight. Bow your head before her. Only a beggar such as you has nothing to lose in this world of plenty.'

I pointed to the mother-to-be and said, 'My sister is in need of a great mother's love such as yours. There will be a newborn.'

She glanced over my shoulder and said, 'Yes, she's not the first and certainly won't be the last to arrive at this door. Do you know what time it is, beggar? Do you even what night it is?'

I raised my hands in the air, but she continued, 'Isn't it perfect timing for a new life?'

She laughed aloud at a beggar with such a gift this night for everyone. I took a step back as the light shone upon the mother-to-be. There was complete silence, then the door of black oak slammed shut. I looked at it with a sense of sadness. How could one's faith be so easily unhinged by such darkness. Especially for a door such as this one of black oak, which, as a sapling, experienced love and kindness that gifted it the strength to be wild and free?

But the light was still on; a glimmer of hope was still there. That was all I ever needed. As the door swung open, a stranger said, 'Follow me, beggar.' And so I did, down a long corridor with nothing but whispers and the odd rattle of keys to keep me company in the night.

I sat in silence as I was told and prayed for forgiveness. The mother-to-be was led further into the darkness, leaving me on my own with just the voices within for company. Not as solitary as it might look to an outsider, but still. There was a kind of smell about the place, a suspicion that I was on tenterhooks just like when a stranger would arrive on my hill of blackthorn. Especially when they were in the right place for the wrong reasons.

'Oh,' the voices spoke up, 'Remember, beggar, to stay silent. Tranquillity is the word for such a place. Being outspoken, as you know well, is bad for business. And such childish thought has no place in our world, lost in the wilderness of Blackthorn Hill.'

'It's who we are,' I thought to myself, and that alone made me sad. I usually had an echo from the valley to answer my call, giving me a lift when I needed it. 'Oh, voices within, you are so right. Not even a baby's cry would be strong enough to reach me in a place like this.'

I stretched out my legs; boredom was beginning to grip them. I pulled them back up to me and let them slide back down again. It was something to do that didn't cost anything. But what really caught my eye was a clock, hanging nearby, for the simple reason that it was working. It had been a long time since I'd seen one. I was always the master of my own time. This clock had a very large hand that looked to be jittering after eleven, waiting for the right moment to strike midnight and bringing with it the smaller hand to signal the beginning of a new day.

I rested my head back and closed my eyes. Mouth opened, I started to snore. I could hear myself snoring but could do nothing about it. I was under the spell of time within this place. But I startled awake at the cry of a child and had a floating sensation as if my spirit had left my body to answer the newborn.

I searched room by room but couldn't locate the source of the cry. A gentle, whispering voice filled the corridors. 'We only ask for one act of kindness, beggar. If your heart desires, set us free. In return, we will gift you a loyalty that will unite all as one. Yes, you, the beggar of Blackthorn Hill, will become the master of all.'

I opened my eyes, but there was nothing beyond they eerie silence. 'Oh, voices within, maybe this is a good time to shoot the breeze in a beggar's language. Out of sight, out of mind. It might be time to head back to our world.'

'Oh,' the voices said, 'I like it. Beggar, we're out of here. Besides, what about Wild Bill? He's probably wondering what's the hold-up.' But the silence was broken as if by a hammer when the sound of snapping footsteps started approaching in my direction.

There was no hiding from such a sound. I am a beggar and had an ear for that kind of thing. As it drew closer, I considered pretending to be asleep. 'No, they have the element of surprise on me. I could always throw myself onto the ground and kick off my shoes. That would be a distraction and would certainly undermine them. Maybe break their focus.'

I dropped my shoulders, cradled my head within my hands, and waited for the arrival of such shoes.

'Oh,' the voices within said, 'You got this one, beggar. Finish them off and show no mercy with the biggest eye. That strength alone will melt an iceberg.'

My beggar's nose picked up a faint scent of perfume, and it was getting stronger.

'Oh,' the voices within said, 'It's a sign of weakness, vanity they call it, self-importance. As if struggling to enjoy life, it's – you've got this one, beggar. Finish them off with your sharp tongue, even though they have the advantage of the wind at their back.'

'Oh,' the voices said, 'Don't worry about it, beggar. It's always been about you. There's nothing you could ever want from such a place – not even from this world. You have it all.' But there was suddenly silence within me.

A towering shadowy figure arrived, maintaining a sociable distance between us – I could feel it in the air. The shadow was out of reach even to my beggar's eye. Whatever was going to be said, I was going to be on the receiving end in this world of years. I would certainly not be on the giving end. I got up and walked behind her. There was nothing to do but let her have the impression that we were not of equal standing while I was in her world.

We came to a sudden stop, and I found myself standing in the middle of a room with a small group of people dressed in white. They hovered over a small baby. 'Look, it's the beggar of Blackthorn Hill,' they whispered and called me over. 'What will you do with this child?'

I replied, 'I'm nothing more than a beggar. I have nothing to offer a child such as this. Many might point at me or even swear an oath upon my name, but few would ever live as I do in this world of plenty.'

The voices continued, telling me that this newborn would never have the strength within to stand with them. Its lifeline was nowhere to be found on the palm of his hand. I checked. All I could see were splendid splashes of colours as if a rainbow of bubbles was arcing from the child's palm. They said, 'It's to be this night of all nights.' And before I knew it, a little tag was placed on the child's ankle, declaring, 'From this day forward, he is to be known as Bubbles.'

I was told to sort it out and make my own way back to the front door. So, I did, passing the room the mother of this child was meant to be. I took another look; in case she might have decided to return. But as darkness gripped the corridors, there was nothing but an echo of light.

Yet, my listening watch was telling me there was someone there; she was back. I wanted to tell her all about the great name that was chosen tonight: Bubbles. Unfortunately, the reality of the situation, was that there was no one there, I'm sorry to say. Only a small figure lying on its back. It was Bubbles, the newborn, covered in a light blanket and struggling to get free. Yes, Bubbles was definitely one of ours. We never like to be tied down, no matter what situation we find ourselves in.

Bubbles' head was tilted to one side, looking away from me because a large mirror had caught his eye. Not even a beggar such as I could hide from such a true reflection. I gazed into it as such warm innocence greeted me. It was as if the sun was rising over my beloved hill of blackthorn. Yes, I was always drawn to power and beauty. Who wouldn't blame me for getting a little closer? And so, I did with a sense of excitement. It was right in front of me, all I had to do was reach out with this hand of strength. But how could I, with such a mirror image from my world? I must look like a monster to this newborn.

The voices within chimed in, saying, 'You're right, my beggar. You are a monster in the eyes of everyone in this world of plenty.' I put my hands up to my face to hide from such innocence.

'Oh,' the voices said, 'Why should you hide? Are you not without shame? Feast your eyes upon this newborn child, flawless in this light that lies before you this night and gifting this world a new splash of splendid colour for everyone to enjoy. But remember, beggar, in our world, when darkness grips within, it's just an illusion. Nothing more than a simple eclipse of the eye, from light to dark, from darkness to an internal light. Such is our life. It has no beginning or end.'

The voices returned, saying, 'What could you ever want from such a child, or even it from you? Are you not the beggar of Blackthorn Hill? Have you not got it all? Was it not always you that kept us united with your hands of strength? Remember what separated us from all kinds of fear. And what's in it for you this night? Nothing. It's all about trust. You are the beggar of Blackthorn Hill, the last of our kind.'

The voices continued, 'We will never let you go, my beggar. You are my eternal love. And what lies before you tonight in this world of plenty will be judged and seen as nothing more than a weakness. Turn your back on this world of suspicion and shame, for such a child. It's a small price for our freedom. We don't belong. Forget about this mirror image of innocence that looks to you. It's not a true reflection of who you really are. You are the beggar of Blackthorn Hill.'

I rested my hand upon the side of the newborn, giving me the lifting strength to rise to my feet. Then, I felt a soft, gentle touch and a sense of forgiveness upon my hand. A calmness had gripped me, silencing the voices within. I looked at the newborn, Bubbles. He grabbed my finger with all his strength and wouldn't let go, giving me a look as if to say, 'Look how you make me sparkle even in the darkest of this night.' That one act of kindness, that glimmer of hope, was all that matters tonight.

I shook my head, searching my recollection of how I lived my life. Maybe only you, Bubbles, could see beyond the madness. As I speak of that night, I'm just a beggar with nothing to offer you. And even if I wanted to change, I didn't know how. I gazed at that little face of innocence, sharing a smile as the singing of a gentle-sounding choir floated through an open window. I knew that song. It had a simple message – 'The Little Drummer Boy.' He, too, had nothing to offer a newborn on a night much like this, except for his kindness and his skill.

A voice whispered to me, 'You know, beggar, even though this child was born into a world that can only ever judge him for who he is, it requires just a single act to demonstrate that the only real things are love and forgiveness from within for who we really are. I heard you whisper these words when you were in the gutter of Angel Lane. Yes, it's easier to carry the weight of forgiveness upon one's shoulders than shame.'

I looked up and noticed the kind face of the woman who had greeted me at the black oak door. She hung a small wooden cross around the newborn's neck and said, 'This was given to me by a sister who is a mother to all. Even though it might have lost some of its magic, it will help him remember a mother's love whenever he gazes upon it. He will bow his head with tears of joy when he hears the voice of an angel sing before he, even though such a he was born into a world with nothing but a great will to live. This alone will unite these two worlds of ours into one. That is, if your heart desires this night.'

Chapter 9

Bubbles

───── ∾ ─────

I t took all my strength to rise to my feet and leave that room, only stopping to reach out with my great hand of strength and give a final nudge to move the hour hand of the clock strike the almighty midnight. It sang out as if it was telling the world, 'This is the beginning of a new day for all kind. This one act of kindness was brought on by nothing more than the strength of a beggar's hand.'

Wild Bill was ready. With one shake of his head, he let me know we were off and heading for the hill of blackthorn. Wild Bill stopped dead in his tracks in front of the old oak door. We watched it disappear behind a new blanket of white. I looked up at the window of darkness and the newborn did the same. I could only smile, knowing that I had stolen its secret for my world, leaving behind nothing but the voices within in this place as I completed this single act of kindness that was asked of me.

Just like that clock, all it ever needed was that helping hand so it could sing with joy. As Wild Bill turned his head to me. I said, 'I couldn't help it.' With a little movement underneath a mother's shawl for company, this newborn known as Bubbles is with us this night. We are one, this child and us, and so be it, as destiny decided a long time ago that this was going to be our chosen path through the Valley of the White Horse. This would surely bring us home to my world at the hill of blackthorn. I tossed the odd glance behind me, hoping to hear a mother calling for her newborn. There was nothing, only an eerie silence. The snow-covered our tracks as if to say, 'Yes, Bubbles, it's just us.'

I thought about what I was going to do with a newborn baby. There was certainly no point in asking Wild Bill. As we started to climb with only a blanket of snow beneath us for comfort, I knew that somebody had given me this child. After all, I am a beggar, and that was what people do. They gave me things that had no value to them, like my beggar's bowl.

'Well, Bubbles, I've only ever had two choices in my life,' I said, giving the newborn the beggar's eye. 'Will I tell you what they are? Take it or leave it. There's nothing else.'

By now, we were approaching the Valley of the White Horse. Wild Bill slowed down. This was his favourite drinking spot. Crystal-clear water flowed from within the hill of blackthorn, and so we drank from it, lifting up Bubbles to show him the wonders of the Valley of the White Horse. The valley's snow-covered trees stood tall and silent long enough to look upon the newborn we had brought into our world. There was no going back. Yes, such a spring was in this newborn now, the same spring that had kept this valley alive and came from deep within the hill of blackthorn. It was all our life's blood, and so it was Bubbles' now, also. As I sprinkled it over his head, I plucked a piece of wild grass and placed it between my thumbs, blowing with all the freshness the valley had to offer on such a night. Its sound echoed across the valley and welcomed Bubbles to this new world of ours, saying, 'There's no turning back for us after this point, Bubbles.'

While looking at the great wood that hid my world from prying eyes, the voice of my dear old friend, the witch, appeared out of the shadows. 'Is that you, my beggar, on a night like this? What have you got there?' As I laid Bubbles onto the ground, she said, 'A child. A new beginning for all that lies between our two worlds tonight. You have no need for such a gift.'

Hearing this, I handed Bubbles to her. I thought she was perfect because she lived on her own. The only friend she'd ever known was the fear that kept her safe even from young, innocent, prying eyes. She would often take out her teeth and wave them in the air at them. She was wise and could answer the call of the tears of a child. She carried Bubbles away within the comfort of her loving, dear old soul, speaking these words of wisdom. 'Don't worry, beggar. When you're ready, Bubbles will stand with you, and climb you will, Blackthorn Hill, as if one. This alone will decide all our fates.'

I found myself back where it all began tonight – stretched out in my bed and thinking that it would be the last time I would open the door in the middle of the night. I looked out my window and listened to the howling winds, searching the valley for any unwanted sounds. Nothing, not even the cry of a newborn. There was only the empty darkness. Hopefully, with the passage of time, this night would be well-forgotten. But, maybe not. Call it a beggar's intuition; it might very well be the start of our story. So be it.

As the snow melted and the magic of spring arrived, giving me a spring in my step to live again, the rose tree flickered and danced with excitement as it was the first to bloom, delivering a scented message of a new season on the horizon.

I hadn't left my hill of blackthorn since that night of Bubble's birth. The fear of losing what I hold so dearly to my heart that night trapped me in my world. I couldn't let it go. It would always be there to answer its call. Would I be missed in a world of plenty? With a heavy heart, I'm fear no one would ever search the shady streets for such a beggar as me. I would be forgotten with the strength of time. I would be as if I never existed. All I can do was rest upon an old, sagging gate that separated our two worlds. I tried to enjoy that moment within time as the seasons came and went. And to be fair, that's all that mattered to me.

As I would look to the sky, I would say, 'I am one lucky beggar.' And there it was, catching my beggar's eye, a sign from my Hill. As if it had just appeared out of nowhere with its blinding colours, my hill of blackthorn was telling me our love was stronger than ever and we would never be separated. Its beauty was a rainbow of splendid colour rising from the hill's peak. Such dazzling colours brought a tear to my eye. 'Why me?' I asked myself. This was too much love, even for a humble beggar such as me. It was a sign of strength, just like me. There was no mistaking it. Only something great like this could appear on top of my hill of blackthorn as if it was reaching out to me. And it would certainly rest at my feet, letting me know I was a hidden little treasure. But it didn't rest at my feet; it passed my gate to the other side. As I followed it with my beggar's eye, I saw it come to rest at the bottom of the hill, landing right outside the witch's house as if my hill of blackthorn was telling me, 'Take a good look, beggar.'

I knew straight away it was Bubbles. He was dressed in black – the only colour of choice. I started to get a flashback of that night, quickly followed by a pain in my head. What was I to do with such a child? Hoping the witch had laid down some ground rules and how things work around here. And it was very simple: what's mine is mine, and no one else's. This gate was a reminder that it stood to separate these two worlds. Any child of mine would get lost in the wilderness of my unforgiving world.

I put my hand up to my eye just to cover the one that had spotted such a child in the first place. Out of sight, out of mind, having the freedom of the other eye to enjoy the view. I was thinking the witch knew that I hated change; it had always been a struggle within me, a distraction perceived as a weakness. Some might see or even call it a friendship, though that meant nothing to me except a huge waste of time.

I spotted a robin sitting on the gate and looking at me, and if I didn't know better, I swear it was the exact Robin I saw the night

Bubbles was born. 'Well, Mr. Robin, there's no point in telling your head or even looking at me. I've done my bit for your world with that one act of kindness for nothing in return. And you certainly won't be catching the beggar twice.' To hell with the lot of them. I closed my door on a very disappointing day. It will be dark shortly, and that will be the end of the rainbow.

When it appeared again, hopefully, it might have changed its colours, and all would be forgiven from my side of the gate. That would be the end of it. Happy ending for all. Well, now all that thinking made the day a little longer than it should be. And when the rose again, there would be no shadow of doubt or even darkness hanging over me. Only brightness and beauty in the perfect world I lived in.

It would be all about the beggar of Blackthorn Hill. With so much time on my hands, I would never miss an opportunity to peel my toenails and flick them into the fire and watch them turn to black ash. The longer they took to burn, the stronger they were. I would always keep the longest toenail. This one would be used to wedge in between my teeth and remove any unwanted food for a midnight snack. Yes, it was always those hidden little treats that I enjoyed the most. Yes, I was a very lucky beggar.

And when tomorrow comes, I will be grand. As I reclined in my chair in a relaxing position and stretched out my feet into the darkness of the night, I thought it was a great plan. I had no problem sleeping on it, and I would serenely rise with the morning sun, opening the door and waiting for such splendid colour. I'm sure I'll be blinded by the tears of such beauty and joy. And rise I did, swinging open my beggar's door and looking at my hill at the centre of my world for inspiration.

But I was blinded with anger. There was nothing, not even a flicker of colour. How could this be? And at that very moment, my hands gripped my side. I remembered what was said to me the night of Bubbles' came to be – this child would unite these two worlds of ours into one, only if the heart desired it.

Yes, I could feel those little shadowy eyes watching me as if a younger version of myself was spying on me from the dark. They were hidden within the colours of my rainbow, which had chosen this newborn, Bubbles, over me and brought him to my gate. I could always raise my blackthorn stick into the air, and that alone would strike fear into anyone. Yes, a rage within, that hidden anger fuelled at the notion of losing my world. That alone would surely make blood boil and give me an uncontrollable fighting spirit.

But, no. That wasn't who I was, and my only reward would be putting myself into a state of darkness. I could end up getting lost and might never find my way back very quickly.

I opened my eyes as I looked at my blackthorn stick. Maybe there was a hidden anger within you that was waiting to get out and strike down all that stood before you. I looked at it as the little robin landed on its tip. Even if one had all the strength and anger in this world, it was no match for the weight of innocence that this little robin contained. All I could do was rest at my gate with a smile on my face when confronted by such innocence. And so be it; I couldn't help it.

After the sun rose every morning, I searched that patch of ground for Bubble's shadow of innocence – even within such blinding colours. Until the morning, there was no rainbow in the sky. Only clouds of darkness. A sadness had covered the house of the witch. She had died and taken with her an air of suspicion and fear that protected my world. It inflicted an element of sadness upon me. She would often say to me, 'The true meaning of life is the one great gift of life itself, to enjoy time within time itself, and nothing else mattered to her.'

As I watched them carry her to her final resting place, I wondered where the shadow of innocence, Bubbles, was. It was not a sign. Maybe the witch was right; I had no use for such a child in my world. I dropped my head and there, right underneath my nose, was Bubbles, staring at me with crystal blue eyes and not even flinching. It was like an unforgiving loyalty I recognized and lived with within the hill of blackthorn.

I said, 'I'm only a beggar and have nothing to offer you, but with all my heart, I welcome you to my world of plenty that will give you everything you desire.' With that, Bubbles walked into my world of free will, climbed upon my gate, and placed his hand on my shoulder. He turned to me, his beggar. 'You are so kind, Bubbles. Every time we see the rainbow, you will think of the witch. Is there anything you want to bring with you from that world of plenty?'

The child greeted me with a smile. 'I have everything in the palm of my hand.'

I gazed upon ia wooden cross, cradled in his palm as if a lifeline between our two worlds. Yes, the same cross that was placed around Bubbles' neck on a night when he had nothing except shadows and darkness for company. 'Will you miss her, Bubbles?'

'No, she is with us now. I can always reach out to her without fear.'

We stopped in our tracks to listen in silence to a chisel striking the limestone that carved her name for into eternity, gifting her the almighty power to outlive all of us who knew of her in this world. And so be it.

'Hi, I'm Bubbles, and this is my big house. I live here. This world of ours gives me everything I could ever want. Even in the darkness, there's always a bright, twinkling star within me. Even the stone slabs that sits under my bare feet glitter as if I was walking upon the night sky. Yes, this is the beggar's house of magic. Its cupboards and shelves are lined with bottles of coloured glass, turned on their heads. My beggar would say to me, "You always find the best at the bottom of the barrel, and why wait for such happiness?" But it was always a treat for me when he would point to one and say, "Try it, Bubbles." And so I would, without question, as its magic would explode in my mouth and my tongue would stick out at the taste of bitterness as if it wanted to run away from my face, shivering from such horror. My beggar would say,

"Is it to your liking, Bubbles?" And I would reply, "Yes, it's perfect." I would never show an ounce of weakness.'

Beneath my beggar's eye, I learned to trust him because there was a reason for everything in his world. Yes, I gained a sense of loyalty to him, stronger than steel and indestructible. Even when there was nothing in the air but bitterness, he would always reward me by saying, 'Bubbles, you're definitely one of ours.' With relaxed facial expression, he would reach for such a taste for himself, looking at me with squeaking watery eyes as he tried to hide the bitterness with a smile. 'Yes,' he would say again, 'You're definitely one of ours. You're nearly ready, Bubbles, for the top shelf, the cream of the crop from a world of plenty.'

I watched the firelight bounce from the bottles to the jam jars, releasing a splendid splash of colours around my beggar's house. I was as if that spark was trying to unite everything together. But, most of all, what caught my eye was his three-legged table. The beggar had sacrificed one to the unending appetite of the fire. He would say it alone had kept it burning, or its faith was certain in my beggar's world and could easily end up in a pile of ashes.

But what rested on the table was his pride and joy – a wooden bowl. It was dearest to his heart. He said, 'It has the power to capture anything from the world of plenty. It shares with me the tales and stories of all the kings and queens that have bowed before it. And someday it will be yours, Bubbles. It will offer you the power of such riches that beggars, tramps, and even thieves will shed tears of joy when they hear you.'

A large spoon appeared from his pocket, which meant only one thing. As he lifted an old lid that sat on a pot, black as the night sky with years of soot, and scooped a white sticky mossy paste down into his wooden bowl. 'Yes,' he would say, 'There's nothing like a simple feast.' But the meal was known to me as crash pandey. Every now and again, the pot of black soot would be topped up with another potato.

They were always on the boil, and he would say, 'What do you think, Bubbles?' Then, he'd stick his finger into it and licking it clean. And I would follow suit, dipping in my middle finger and saying, 'Just right, my beggar. It's perfect.'

'Yes, Bubbles, we don't need any parties up here on this hill of blackthorn, as every day is a birthday. Here, we scream and shout with such delight and free will for everyone to hear.' My beggar would jump to his feet with such joy. 'Yes, I love my beggar's house. It's like having a birthday every day.' We jumped around as the two spiders would arrive in all their glory, sitting on their pride and joy and watching with prying eyes with their front row seats.'

Yes, my beggar was larger than life itself. But he could slip into the shadows of the house as if he was never there, only to reappear out of nowhere. Yes, this house had no sense of time. It was as if time itself had stopped, giving me the greatest gift of all – I, Bubbles, am the centre of my beggar's universe. Yes, he would say to me, 'We will enjoy time within time itself.'

He often asked me to remind him of my age.

'I don't know,' I'd say in a voice of shame.

'Don't worry, Bubbles, on Blackthorn Hill, it's always been mind over matter.' He laughed aloud and said, 'Do you know why, Bubbles?'

'No,' I replied.

'I will tell you. I don't mind, so it doesn't matter in my world of blackthorn. And so be it, let's be twelve today, and when the sun rises tomorrow, you can be ten, and a very strong ten you can be.'

I asked my beggar to look at the palm of my hands and tell me what he saw. 'You have the hands of an angel; a gift from the Almighty. Whoever follows its lifeline will be rewarded with an eternity of happiness.'

I looked at them and said, 'You can see all that, my beggar?'

'Yes, Bubbles, you've got the greatest gift of all. You have the will to live a life in a world that will give you everything your heart desires, just like me.' I gazed at his hands; they were strong hands, forged with nothing but the love of time. They would always be by my side; I could trust them with my life. Tears of joy rested upon my cheeks, and I knew I was finally home.

My beggar said, 'What's the matter with my hands? Why do they make you sad?'

'Nothing, my beggar, they're tears of joy, not sorrow,' I said. He grabbed me and gently lifted me over his head as if I was being carried by nothing more than a breeze. It felt as if I had wings so strong that they could split even the hardest of hearts. As we would always come crashing down onto a raggedy old couch, he shouted to the heavens, 'I nearly lost you there, Bubbles,' which made us laugh.

'You know there's a price to be paid for everything, and there's nothing for nothing in this world of ours,' he said, stretching out his fingers. 'Yes, there's a story to be told with every one of them that would send a shiver down your spine.' His mighty hand towered over my face, the fingers blocking the light from all except for a single gap. My beggar was missing a finger. In its place was a fiery flame.

'Oh, Bubbles,' he said in a deep voice, 'I lost it on the hill of blackthorn many years ago, a day I'll never forget. It was taken from me by the puck goat that lived on the crossroads of the four winds. No one could escape his scent of fear, and he always rose to the occasion. He'd rear up on his back legs and challenge anyone who dared to invade his home and would face them down. He did the same to me, the beggar of Blackthorn Hill. The goat lunged at me with all his strength and tried to push me over the cliff's edge. All I could do to save my life from a certain death was to shove my hand in his mouth and hang onto his bitter tongue. As he bit down, off went my finger. It was gone, and he stood back from me with a wink from his eye as if to say, "Oh, how sweet a fall from grace is." He watched me chew my own finger and swallowed it whole. But I had to spit it out onto the ground. It had nothing within except the bitter taste of who I am. He bowed his head to me, letting me pass without awe. Only a man with such strength could live a life in such a place as Blackthorn Hill.'

'Oh, my beggar, will I lose a finger to such fear of not knowing where I belong?'

'I don't know, but don't worry. Just like me, you have another nine to spare.' I quickly put my hand into my pocket and my beggar noticed this. 'Well, Bubbles, he might see something even stronger in you than a finger, and you could be one of the lucky ones. But whatever it is, he will find it and bow his head to you for who you are, and he will always let you pass. Just like me.'

'Where is your finger now?'

'It's lost in the hill of blackthorn to remind me that even a beggar such as I can lose something of great value.' Having a good look at each other, my beggar looked longer at my hands and shook his head. 'I don't know, Bubbles. Is this the place for you? This world of mine?'

'Take another look, my beggar.'

'I don't know,' he said. 'They look very soft and tender to me.'

'Look at them again, my beggar,' I said with a determined voice of strength. 'Maybe there's something there.' I looked at his hands and he looked at mine. 'What can you see?'

'You're nearly there. You'll be one of ours yet, with a beggar's grip. And anyone who challenges you for living such a life will shiver with fear at such a grip, even in the hottest of days. Yes, tomorrow we will climb the hill of blackthorn together as one. You never know; we might find my missing finger. That will be something for all.'

He relaxed on his old chair, which had a cushion of rope crisscrossed in all directions as if it was a spider's web. It was a perfect fit for a man such as my beggar. 'Can you hear it, Bubbles? The whistling of the wind. It usually tells me a new story with the coming of nightfall. But tonight, it sings to me. Such a joyful sound.' He fell asleep within this house of shadows.

I watched over him, his bare feet rested upon the cold stone floor to keep them cool. Yes, his feet carried him with such pride and strength – everything that he held dear. His hands lay across his chest as if they were great protectors of his heart. The only way to get to it was that small space created by his missing finger. Maybe someday I could fit within that space that had such great value to him.

His face was hidden from the world with a white beard with a tinge of yellow. His hat had seen better days, scorched from the blistering sun and tilted forward. It rested against his nose, keeping everything within its place. He was mine; my beggar. I watched a misty steam rise from his clothes only to be taken away by a breeze as if it was waved away by a great mother's hand. I'll never let him go; he is my beggar, and I wasn't alone. His two spiders were by my side, their eyes glittering from the fire. I could see it in them; they were the keepers, with such loyalty to this house of the beggar of Blackthorn Hill.

I settled across the old couch, falling into a deep sleep under their watchful spell until I was startled awake by him calling, 'Bubbles? Bubbles, where are you? Get up, Bubbles.' I rubbed my eyes and opened them. I found myself looking into my beggar's mouth, which was full of cracked teeth. What came flying out filled me with excitement. 'I'm starving, Bubbles.' Then, with a little whisper in my ear, 'It's breakfast time,' and with one mighty scoop, he splashed pandey for everyone to enjoy. 'Get that into you, Bubbles; it will put hair on your chest. You'll be ready to climb the hill of blackthorn.'

Chapter 10

The Hill of Blackthorn

'I'm ready, my beggar.'

'Yes, this is a celebration. Let's release the bag of cats for all to hear just as my father did for me when I climbed the hill of blackthorn for the first time. They're locked up over there in an old trunk. Every time I take them out, Bubbles, there's no bitterness. There's only sweetness in their voices.'

I couldn't take my eyes off the trunk. 'Imagine. There have been cats in there since his father's time,' I thought, 'They must be very old; maybe even hungry.'

'We'll get them out, Bubbles, and make them scream in a way that hasn't been heard before. Everyone will hear them from miles around,' he said, 'There's a new set of eyes on Blackthorn Hill.'

I watched as he made his way over to a shadowed corner of the house. He said, 'Where are they hiding? It's been a while. Don't worry, Bubbles; I'll get them out.'

'Yes,' I said, 'Get them out.' Before I knew it, he fell to his knees in front of the old trunk, and with one intake of air that filled his lungs, he raised his head as if he was looking at the sky. With one mighty blow, a cloud of dust rose into the air, filling my beggar's house and obscuring him. He disappeared into a dusty cloud of particles as if he was a flame snuffed out. Only when the dust settled was it quite clear that the centre of this new universe was the old wooden chest and what it contained. All that separated us from its contents was a lock, which hung with a stillness that I interpreted as a hidden sense of pride. It didn't care that time itself had forgotten it. 'Oh, my beggar,' I said, jumping to my feet. 'I want to see them and hold them! I'm ready, I want to hold them.'

'Why not?' said my beggar as he tugged at the old lock. There wasn't a stir. It was as if it was resting in my beggar's palm for a brief moment, stubbornly questioning him, 'Are you sure this is worthy of a celebration for all to hear?' As the dust settled in silence and relished in its stubbornness, my beggar turned to me and said, 'I'll strike it for you, Bubbles.' Before I knew it, he had ripped it from its hinges goosed the lock at his feet. It never had a chance when it came to my beggar's strength. With a wink of his eye, he said, 'Nothing should ever get in the way of true happiness.'

He lifted the lid. Before I knew it, my beggar's head had disappeared into the old trunk like he had been swallowed whole. I heard a faint screeching sound. I took a step back, maybe they were really angry for being locked in the trunk for so long. Given half a chance, they might try to sink their claws into the first living thing that appeared before them. Perhaps even in celebration of their newfound freedom. But I didn't care. 'Give them to me, my beggar. Why are they hiding?' I asked. 'I want to hold them.'

'Don't worry, Bubbles; you'll get them.'

Before I knew it, a sound emanating from the trunk spread to the floor right in front of me like a blight. But there were no cats. It looked to me like a woolly bag that changed colour as my beggar's had gentle swept across it. I looked to my beggar and he explained, 'These are the bagpipes of Blackthorn Hill, woven together like one of them had strayed from their path and could never find their way back. They give her the means to capture the spirits well beyond her horizon with such a strong siren song that not even you, Bubbles, could resist their call.

They will let us know our path has been chosen for us to climb the hill of blackthorn. Are you ready?'

'Yes, my beggar,' I said as he stood up and tucked the bag of such a calling underneath one arm, holding the blackthorn stick under the other. He lifted me onto his shoulders. 'No, Bubbles, this is where a new king should always sit. On a throne that gives you the freedom and strength to live your life in the public's eye. Now, Strike the door of the beggar's house with all your strength, Bubbles, and let's enjoy its welcoming echo as if it has been a long time since it received a guest.' And so I did, and I could hear its echo filling the valley, announcing the arrival of a new friendship. With that, the beggar pulled the bolt across and whispered to me, 'As long as you live in this house, you will stay here. This is the greatest gift of all – the freedom to celebrate within Blackthorn Hill.'

With one mighty intake of his breath, he placed the blackthorn pipe in his mouth, resting his fingers on it. I knew this was going to be the calling that I could never be able to resist. Closing my eyes and raising my hands into the air as the pipes sang aloud, I could feel its giggling power within birth a loyalty to me. Opening my eyes, I was spinning within my beggar's house, surrounded by splendid colours as a rainbow, lifting that bitter taste lingering on my beggar's shelf.

The door flung open with an explosive release out to the hill of blackthorn. Not even swarms of sparrows could resist such a calling. It was a wildness that would always live within me, such freedom I would enjoy in this world. Yes, I realised I was home as my beggar looked at me and said, 'When I was little, just like you, I also sat where you are sitting now on my father's shoulders. And now, if this is your chosen path, it will always bring you home to Blackthorn Hill.

We stopped to greet the fresco known to all as the Tears of Our Lord, standing guard against whoever dares to enter this world, easily turning those who show no response for this place to tears of sadness and sorrow. Tomorrow, with the crack of dawn, we will take this path together with the rising of the sun.

As I sat with my beggar and watched him drift away into his world where there was no sense of time, a new day arrived before we knew it. It did so with the calling of our two-legged friend, Cock, and their heaving that voice that prompted one to rise with the dawn. The wake-up call let us know this was going to be our finest hour as a blazing fire crested with such a light. It sent a trail of smoke up and out into the sky, which was whipped away by a strong north westerly wind as if she was blowing in our favour this day – her strength at our backs.

'Oh, my Beggar, I have no shoes,' I said before we set off.

'It doesn't matter in this world of ours; you will be grand.'

We passed a tree of roses in full bloom, a welcome sign of an early spring with its blinding splash of colour. 'Remember, Bubbles, such a greeting can carry bitterness within as if time twisted the tree's trunk and titled its spirit to one side. Remember, Bubbles, when passing through their arched branches heavy with roses, its beauty is only in the eyes of the beholder. You most likely will never see what lies deep within its heart.'

My beggar waved at me and then pointed down. 'Look to its roots; they have broken through all twisted and bitter with such anger towards anything that passed over them. For the living, their lives exist within the shadows of such beauty, skipping over them with such tenderness and respect despite never knowing such beauty, only to be greeted with the sweet smell of clove fields.'

Yes, spring bloomed the air with every colour you could dream of, but my beggar knew this place. He told me that such a place could only be admired from a distance since what lies within is nothing more than a delusion of happiness – a bed of thorns. When crossing its narrow path, we stayed within the shadow of the cliff with the gentle touch of Mother Nature's helping hand. He warned that all could be lost to a blinding sun, sending one over the cliff's edge to meet the skull cracker.

We watched it rise before us in a blaze of glory. We had made it to the top of Blackthorn Hill and stood on an old flagstone.

'This is our world, Bubbles. As far as the eye can see.' My beggar pointed to the distant land with its blood-red sky. It looked like a world gone mad with a hunger. Not even the rising of a tide could quench such a thirst; it would surely destroy this world we called home. The beggar told me that we would strike them down when the time was right, and Blackthorn Hill called on us to do so. He raised his hands into the air. 'Can you feel her power beneath us, Bubbles?'

'Yes.'

'A swelling, lifting wind of strength will raise us from such a noisy world containing nothing but greed, and we will set it ablaze. We will watch it burn from this very spot while the blackthorn bushes whistle in the wind. We're ready to fight with our prodding thorns; yes, they will unite and stand with us until the bitter end. Bubbles, it takes great will to live a life here, where we call home. But it gives me everything that our hearts desire.'

I plucked a white piece of grass and placed it between his thumbs. With his lips, he produced a calling sound that lifted the spirits of all. 'See, you have nothing to fear; we are one.' As my beggar pointed to the great wood of hazel that protected this world of his with its whispering voices of fear, he said, 'To all, Blackthorn Hill is the land of the beggars. Only you, Bubbles, can decide to take this path.'

He left me standing alone. While I looked at the ground, I could see a stretching shadow reaching for me. I shouted aloud to my beggar, but he was gone, leaving me alone to make this choice. I could only feel that hidden sense of anger deep within my heart for never knowing a mother's love, which gave me this great gift of life and this anger was telling me to run for eternity and live in this world of blame.

As I closed my eyes and took a deep breath and searched my soul, I remembered the pure magic that was given to me by my humble beggar. Words of wisdom. To never look behind you with anger, as the past might blind, and you might never see the true brightness of the light within. As I opened my eyes with tears of joy, I shouted, 'I see everything.' I was steeped within this world of shadows and whispers for all to see as the trees towered over me like they originated from a distant land.

I could hear chatting, creaking, whispering voices of wisdom surrounding me. As I stood in silence among such giants with what seemed to be integrity, but in my heart, I knew my life was nothing more than a fallen leaf to them. But this is my home now, just like my beggar. We would watch over him and place a fallen star within his heart and watch it grow as if we were one.

I walked along the beds of bluebells and watched them ring out in silence with every gust of wind as if celebrating this path I had chosen that would surely bring me home to my beggar. I said to my beggar, 'This was a great day,' as I drifted into this new world of mine.

Before I knew it, I was shaking my beggar, trying to wake him up.

'Where did the time go, Bubbles?' he asked as I looked up at the little figure standing in front of me. 'You remind me of myself, standing there all dressed in black with a hat perched upon you. Oh, how you remind me of myself when I was your age.'

'Do I, beggar?'

'Yes'

'Let's climb the hill of blackthorn.'

'Oh, Bubbles, this old beggar doesn't need to rise to such an occasion. I can see everything through your eyes. It's a gift within time itself as if just one long bay that we can enjoy together.' He stopped and pointed at me with such innocence, 'Bubbles, where are your shoes?'

'Gone missing. Like yours, my beggar. But don't worry, I can do lots of things without them. I can pick up things with my toes and put them in my mouth. I might not ever wear shoes again, my beggar. But most of all, I can feel the soil of Blackthorn beneath my feet. Oh, such a sparkle! I can certainly light up the night sky.'

'Enough, Bubble. You are blinding me with such delight. I might never see my hill of blackthorn again. Yes, this is a great life, and I've wanted for nothing. I wear my clothes in bed if I want to. And sometimes, when I wash my hair, it changes colours like leaves in the depth of autumn. I can fly like the wind and pluck from the rose tree without fearing hidden bitterness in retaliation. I can rest my head upon their bed of thorns without even a scratch. I can cross the narrow pass as if I was swallow, running the tips of my wings along her cliff's edge, never in blinding fear of the skull cracker. I can rise, and I would, to the top of my hill of blackthorn with the wind to my back as if it was chasing me, stretching out my limbs and capturing her love upon my face. She lifts me into the sky. It's as if to say, "We've got you, Bubbles, and will never let you go."'

I watched the evening sky turn blood red over a world that never sleeps; it was as if it was searching for me. I shot a breeze within a dust cloud that would carry me home. There was never any doubt about where home was. I could see a meandering line of smoke peeking out over the treetops as if it were calling me. What more do I want out of life? But I never looked behind me like it was a long-ago learned golden rule. As if breaking it would result in some punishment to the world that rested beneath such a red sky. But I'd always stop to admire the wild roses hidden by their thorns, out of reach even for me. I could only lean forward to steal their scent of beauty.

Oh, how safe they were even when surrounded by such danger. I was also never alone. I sensed things in the corner of my eye as if something or someone was watching over me. It was nothing more than a snap of a twig, a leaf crossing my path for no reason, or even a gentle shake of a bush. I could feel it from the ground up, conveyed through my bare feet. I knew I was not alone on this hill of blackthorn. But I could only hear my beggar calling me, with a listening watch. He always knew where I was, even when he thought I was lost. But not to fear, I followed those sounds of Mother Nature. She would always lead me back to the one place – my beggar's house, a picture of beauty to me.

As I stood on the flagstone outside Blackthorn Hill with my bare feet, always waiting for me without question, I closed my eyes and felt its calmness to the touch. It gave me a deep sense of happiness. It was telling me that nothing mattered beyond this world. Not even time itself.

Inside, the open fire captured my imagination. Its light bounced from bottle to bottle, searching for my beggar's hidden treasures, providing a new sense of delight. And there my beggar sat, with his eyes closed and nothing but an old sweeping brush resting by his side, even though it had lost its magic to sweep as life had worn it down. But that didn't matter to my beggar since this was its rightful place. 'Well, how was your day, Bubbles?' my beggar asked, and I prepared to tell my story. But not before taking my rightful place alongside my beggar, stretching out my legs and wiggling my toes, not a sock on between us.

'My beggar, I can feel the hill of blackthorn as if it's watching me all the time.'

'I know that feeling, Bubbles. It's a friendship that can last a lifetime. It will always look upon you with a sense of pride in who you are and where you belong.'

'But, my beggar, when I climb the hill of blackthorn to rest on its peak and I look to that distant land with its blood-red sky, I wonder, does it ever sleep? Does it enjoy its night sky? And someday, will it steal our sparkle?' We gazed into the fire with my questions weighing on our minds.

'Well, Time has taught me that the older we are, the wiser we become. We must accept things more graciously,' said my beggar. He pointed to a wooden log covered in moss. 'Yes, soft to the touch, like our world, but happy to live in peace and enjoy each other's company. Place it in the fire.'

I moved it there and it sat with pride of place for everyone to enjoy for a brief moment. Soon, the flames started to rise and engulfed everything. The life treasures it enjoyed could not escape such a fate. I looked at my beggar. 'Do you think there is an escape from such a fate?'

'No, Bubbles, even I don't have the strength to save them. That world we speak of will surely destroy ours and everything that we love. Remember this night, Bubbles. Every flame has to have its own spark. Even my brother's hand, though he lies underneath its blood-red sky, blinded by its power.'

'Don't worry. We might be the last of our kind, but you will strike a new spark within this world of his and save Blackthorn Hill when the time is right. It will be a new beginning for all, just like what you have given me.'

But I couldn't take my eyes off that log. It was as if Blackthorn Hill was being consumed by flames; no mercy was shown for that place called home by everyone. 'Don't worry, my beggar. I won't be blinded by bright lights like your brother. They'll never see me coming underneath the shadows of darkness.'

As we laughed aloud, he said, 'Imagine that. Such a fate lies within your hands. Yes, you, Bubbles. And when the time is right, you will save Blackthorn Hill.'

Then, there it was. A scratching sound I had been waiting for. I had caught a mouse in a bottle that had been resting against my beggar's door. Oh, such a mouse! He couldn't resist such a treasure and went sliding down the bottle to have a feast fit for a king. I had him; he was mine – that mouse trapped in the bottle. 'Look, my beggar, I have a new friend.'

As the mouse looked out at us, quite content with the situation he found himself in and had decided it was what it was, he continued to enjoy his feast. 'Look at him, my beggar. He's not even frightened. Maybe he knows something we don't. Maybe he has some advantage over us. I wonder, my beggar, what could it be? Do you think he has many brothers or sisters? Will they miss him?'

My beggar gave him a little shake to him know we were talking about him. 'You know, Bubbles, his family are probably saying he's gone on a holiday somewhere far away. But I only have him for a few minutes, which is no time at all.'

'Yes, my beggar, but that could be a lifetime to him. Imagine that, a mouse on a holiday.'

As we watched him nibble away and leave nothing behind, my beggar said, 'He is having a right good holiday. He's at the best one – all-you-can-eat and free. I gave him another little shake to say hello and that his holiday was over. I let him go; his mother might be looking for him. 'Yes,' said my beggar, 'That's the hardest part for anyone – letting go.'

We spent the evening talking about the mouse and the wonderful holiday he had. But such joyful chat stopped suddenly when the Night Walker would approach the house. I always knew when he was coming. He had no sense of direction – his cod eye that always led him astray – and he always ended up in the field with Wild Bill, thinking he was in the company of my beggar.

Oh, how he loved the sound of his own voice. When anyone offered him a kind ear, they would get his life stories without him ever taking a breath.

Wild Bill would cock his tail in fright and bellow at him. Then, there would be silence, not a sound, as if death was in the air. My beggar would laugh and make his way to window with a gentle tapping sound.

This gave my beggar a little time to lock the door if he was not in the right frame of mind for such a calling. But to be fair, my beggar was always in a good mood when he thought of the fright Wild Bill got as the Night Walker told him his life story. It didn't matter; like I said, the door was never locked. My beggar always said, 'The flagstones shouldn't have a heart of stone.'

With one swing of the door, the Night Walker was inside, arriving in all his glory. I watched his wandering eye search for a place to rest, making sure to stay out of his path since he had a habit of grabbing me and raising me up, leaving my legs dangling and rubbing his stubbly chin against my face.

'Now, Bubbles, you've gotten a bit more colour in your cheeks since I last saw you.' He dropped me onto the ground without concern. 'Well, beggar, is that you I see there?' He laughed heartily as I rubbed my cheek.

He might be the Night Walker to my beggar, but I had my own name for him – Hairy Jaws. Landing himself in front of the fire and kicking off his shoes, he said, 'Well, Bubbles, how do you like it on this side of the hill?' He winked to my beggar. What he really meant was, 'Have you fallen into the Valley of the White Horse?' I looked at him, trying to catch his eye. I believed I could cross it with one eye even if the other one got lost.

'I'm glad to hear such a tale, Bubbles, and that this place is in safe hands,' he said as my beggar nodded to me. But the Night Walker always carried a shadow of darkness within him.

'Yes, the Night Walker was always full of stories. When he passed through the Valley of the White Horse, collecting such tales and delivering them to us, without a shadow of a doubt,' my beggar said as I sat next to him.

Hairy Jaws, as I called him, was small in stature with a stubble face, sunken cheekbones, a pointed nose, and a set of shifty eyes that always ended up staring at me with an air of suspicion. 'Yes,' he said to my beggar, 'I made it across the Valley of the White Horse.' He struck his chest with his hand as if to say, 'I had to kickstart my heart; it stopped while in the valley, with such a fright.'

Conversations with Hairy Jaws were quick fire: 'Beggar, is Bubbles really something to name a child?' and, 'Oh, the Valley of the White Horse. There aren't many who can tell such a story like me, isn't that right, you old beggar?' and, 'And how it got its name? Well, Bubbles, it's a meadow rich in soil. Many have gazed upon the fields that run as far as the eye can see, rewarding whoever works it with a plentiful harvest. Oh, such riches from Mother Nature.'

But knowing Hairy Jaws, he never had a happy ending to any of his tales, and there would be no escape for me. Even if I closed my eyes, I could feel his power over this tale as the Night Walker reached his hand toward me.

There was to be no escaping such horror as I looked upon the cuts, bruises, and scars that cover him as if he had fought off a wild animal. I closed my eyes in shock; these were the hands that picked me up and might even take me away in the dead of night to such a place. Yes, the Valley of the White Horse, once a field of dreams and beauty and a pleasure for all to see. But hidden in the corner was an altar of devoted to the hand of Mother Nature within such a field.

At the altar, many offerings were made over the years - bread and wine even during a famine or drought, hoping she would look on those who tended her fields even during the harshest of times. But a blistering sun had fallen upon them. On such a day, looking up to see if there was shelter and only spotting the altar that seemed to call to them and welcome them to rest, they sat beneath her shade with peace of mind.

Except for one. A gripping thirst had overpowered him, and, looking to the altar, found the offering of a bottle of red wine. He couldn't resist such sparkling riches and drank from it until he was satiated as the altar shook with such anger, shouting at him, 'I welcomed you and gave you shade, peace of mind, and yet you steal from me with such unclean hands. Let it be known from this day forward that those hands and feet will always carry this field within them, turning him into a white horse, even in the darkest of nights. Give him a plough to pull as a reminder for eternity. You will have to carry it upon your shoulders since you disrespected the great hand of

Mother Nature. You will plough this field of dreams into nothing more than a harsh valley of jagged stone that nobody can bear to cross.'

Many had heard the rattling chains of that plough before. Hairy Jaws started to laugh, raising his hands to show me. 'Look into them, Bubbles. Maybe I am the plain man that escaped such a fate just to sit with you and the beggar of Blackthorn Hill.'

But was there another story with Hairy Jaws' hand? He placed his thumb into his palm, moving it around. It made a crushing sound like walking on crispy leaves, then there was silence. All I could do was wait and watch until he opened his palm.

With a sense of relief, I realised it was tobacco. He had ground it down to a fine powder for his pipe; he filled it and struck a match. I watched it come back to life as a line of smoke stretched into the night air as if it were searching for me with its new sense of freedom. Not even the heavy hand of the Night Walker could crush something that was meant to be free on Blackthorn Hill.

'Cheers to all a simple pleasure,' he said. He drank from one of the jam jars of splendid colours, releasing their spirits into the night to laugh and sing and dance joyfully. But when he rose to his feet, he did so with a creaking of his knees amidst a howling wind. 'It's time for me to go,' he announced, winking at me. 'I hate to be caught out among the riches in the Valley of the White Horse with this wandering eye of mine.'

Early summer was upon us. The nights were getting shorter, and the evenings longer, which meant the arrival of the swallows from a distant land, tilting their wings in such a way that announced to everyone the arrival of summer in all its glory, lifting our spirits. I spotted my beggar in a dust cloud out in the field, mowing Wild Bill's hair. He would look to me but never call; there was no point. Such a calling would never be strong enough to set me free from my hill of blackthorn.

'I hear you, Bubbles,' he said.

'How did you know it was me?'

With a sense of disappointment, he opened his eyes and looked up at me. 'I had a little help from Mother Nature. She tilted it in my favour. The crickets fell silent, giving you away.'

I handed him a jam jar of tea I brought and took my rightful place. I sat with my beggar and drank from our splash of delight. 'And what surprise did you get?'

'Well, I got marmalade. What about you, Bubbles?'

'Honey.'

My beggar counted the flies that landed within our splash and then tossed them down the hatch. My beggar said, 'Not to fear, Bubbles. They're going to a better place with a sweet taste in their mouths, gulping them down.'

And so I followed his lead with a wink of my eye.

'And what flies escape from such a sweet-tasting fate will be captured by the swallows. This is life, Bubbles,' he said to me. Even the crickets had recovered from their silence and filled the air once again, chirping amongst themselves.

'Do you know, my beggar, what they speak of?'

'I know exactly what they're saying, Bubbles. You'll never get one over on the beggar of Blackthorn Hill while they're watching my back.'

No, it was the threat of rain that my beggar feared the most, that dark line of clouds along the horizon. He would say to me, 'You never know when the heavens will open,' and it would certainly steal all beneath us. Checking the sky for such darkness, my beggar pointed to a strange shadow of darkness that seemed to dropped from the sky.

He said, 'Well, Bubbles, what do you think of such darkness?'

I knew what my beggar was asking me. This was going to be the greatest test of all to see if we were of one mind and soul. Could I see this world through the eyes of my beggar of Blackthorn Hill, which had given him everything his heart desired? Many had looked upon it with nothing more than a glare of suspicion. I faced my beggar's expression of kindness, hoping this would give me the strength to answer this calling. Yes, this was the greatest test of all for me. I could hear our hearts beat in synchronicity. I knew every cut and crack upon his strong that reached for me that night with nothing but his act of kindness in this world of shadows and suspicion that would only ever judge me and never see me for who I really am.

I could only gaze upon him with such beauty, even though his chosen path had left nothing more than scars upon his face that were filled with tears of sorrow for a world that never sleeps. My beggar of Blackthorn was hidden from such a fate. Maybe someday, they might look upon him with envy for living his life in a world that gave him everything his heart desired. Oh, those facial expressions. There was no hiding from me. I could read them as if they were the seasons all rolled into one, each telling their own story but none a true reflection of my beggar. I always captured the windows to his soul for myself and gave him the greatest gift of all – living with him as a part of this world of blackthorn that he calls home and asking for nothing in return. I do so, as great minds think alike.

We turned our backs on the approaching shadows, as I'm sure they would never be able to cross the Valley of the White Horse. 'Yes,' he said to me, laughing jollily. 'It's our way or the highway to them, Bubbles. After all, I am a beggar with no sense of time.'

He cast his eyes up to Blackthorn Hill. 'Can you smell it, Bubbles? There it is, the cracking-scented smell of youthfulness that always follows you. It has the power, Bubbles, to take you back to when you were at your happiest. Such a scent can be found in the most distant of lands, setting the stage for you. Not even you can resist such a calling.'

My beggar turned and looked at the reek of hay. 'For Wild Bill, a feast fit for a king. This should get him through the winter months. And Blackthorn Hill will look after the rest of your needs.' And with that, my beggar was up and gone. I watched the white misty dew descend upon me like a mother's love for a lost child when I heard my beggar's voice calling me. I whispered to the mist, 'Until we meet again,' and then headed for home, taking my place by the welcoming fire.

'Aren't we blessed, Bubbles?' he said to me, looking at his great set of hands. 'And how they work together as one, making the day a little lighter. Are they not a great invention?'

I replied, 'If they could only talk, what do you think they would say?'

'Well, Bubbles, I'm sure such fingers would say, "Take it or leave it."'

'You're probably right.'

My beggar stretched out his feet and kicked off his shoes, sending them flying in all different directions. It wouldn't surprise my beggar if one ended up in the fire. With a hearty laugh, he said to me, 'Don't they all look the same, yearning for the flames? And now they're trying to put me to sleep. Who needs love in their lives when you have shoes like that? And there's plenty more of them where that one comes from.'

The summer evenings gave way to winter nights, always seeming to arrive before their time as if an early changing of the guard that was bitter towards all things living. Its swollen winds would rise before me, stripping everything of their beauty and laying it at my feet.

I stood within hazelwood, and I felt her roaring power descend upon me. 'Yes,' I would shout out to her, 'We are one and the last of our kind to live in a place such as Blackthorn Hill.'

I spied on the shadows creeping into the Valley of the White Horse but could only watch them in silence underneath a cover of darkness.

My beggar called on me and my nimble fingers to tune his radio for that perfect sound. He said, 'You can do it, Bubbles. Your fingers have the gentle touch and can slowly turning that chunky knob.'

I pulled up the first station. 'Is it that one, my beggar?' His only reply was a dismissive wave of his hand. I turned my head to him in a silent challenge as if to say, 'That was a good one, my beggar,' but his response was a slight shake of his head with his two eyes closed. When a sound of pleasure reached his ear, his hands flew in all directions as to say, 'Stand back from the wireless, Bubbles.' It was like fear of losing the station had overcome him. I tried to set the volume for him, but he jumped up from his chair and grabbed his blackthorn stick.

'Louder,' he said to me, demanding that I deliver on such a stage as if a sudden stop would surely kill him.

He let out a scream. 'My hill of blackthorn is on fire and it's calling us to save it. Get up upon my back, Bubbles.'

I did and hung on for dear life. 'I've got your back, my beggar. We are one.'

He waved his blackthorn stick in the air. 'Yes, Bubbles, it's just us against the whole world.' With one mighty swing, the blackthorn stick came crashing down onto the table and lifted everything into the air as if gifting them wings or an escape for them from such a fate.

I could feel his power and anger like an untamed rage. Then silence, not a sound except his heart beating a perfect rhythm. At that very moment, the door swung open, breaking the silence. He screamed, 'It's now or never, Bubbles,' as we turned to face our demons together, only to realise it was Hairy Jaws standing there. He turned on his heels and went flying down the hill, shouting to all in the distance, 'The beggar has gone mad!'

We collapsed onto the ground. 'You know, Bubbles, it's the curse of Blackthorn Hill. It's a tale that has been handed down through the generations. Now, it rests in me like a poison that runs through my veins. I can't help it. The longer I live, the stronger its fiery spirit gets. Yes, Bubbles, I remember such a tale as if it were this night. Can you hear its heartbeat, Bubbles? It lies beneath these flagstones we're resting on. Oh, such a spirit belonged to a great Celtic chieftain, conqueror of all. He had such a hand of fear and cruelty that everyone bowed before him. All but one. He heard tales of a beauty in a distant land, with crystal blue eyes, skin as pale as snow, and hair that flowed from upon her shoulders covered in silver and gold. A fitting Queen for such a chieftain.

'And rise he did. With his great army gathered upon these very cobblestones, he said, "Go forward, and whoever captures her beauty and brings it to me will be rewarded with land as far as the eye can see." But I could only watch in horror as over the cliff's edge they pushed and shoved, blinded by such riches and screamed aloud for such a loss, for all dear to him. Out of desperation, he fell to his knees and ordered the hill to be set alight, as if, "If I can't capture such beauty, no man will." And watch it burn from this very cobblestone. But she did rise to such a calling. With her great hand of nature, she captured his fiery flames within her mighty breath, burning all to a pile of ash and gifting him an eternity of love for such loyalty to her.

'This house was built as a reminder. Only someone with such loyalty could ever rest upon its cobblestones. Yes, Bubbles, even death is not the end. It's the beginning of a new life.'

Little did we know, as I listened to my beggar's tale of the curse of Blackthorn Hill, Hairy Jaws was telling another story to whoever had a kind ear for him. He claimed the beggar had gone mad with a child called Bubbles on his back and he was fighting with the demons of Blackthorn Hill with his Blackthorn stick. 'I was in fear for my life;,' he said, 'The hill has taken his soul like all before him.'

As everyone listened with an eerie, deafening silence, they spoke between themselves. 'This is the beggar of Blackthorn Hill we are talking about. Who among us will dare to stand in front of him and strike him down?'

They turned and looked at Hairy Jaws, asking, 'But what of the child? Yes, we will save him from the beggar's fate, but to hell with the beggar and his demons. Leave him where he belongs, lighting up the sky with torches of fire!'

They pointed at Hairy Jaws. 'Lead us across the Valley of the White Horse; this will bring us to the house of the beggar.'

As dusk fell and gripped the valley, Hairy Jaws turned to the charging mob. 'Maybe this night is not for me.' The beggar pushed me to one side as the night sky lit up, catching his attention. 'Look, Bubbles. The sky is on fire.'

As we rose from the cobblestone, our fighting spirit burning within, we watched as a serpent of fire crisscrossed the Valley of the White Horse. 'You smell that, Bubbles? Hatred for our world is in the air. They're no better than the great chieftain's army, blinded by their greed. What do they want? Something of great value that I got from one act of kindness asked of me? That will save us all from a world of greed. You can never capture something meant to be free.'

'We meet them at the rose tree and let the hill of blackthorn decide all our fates. Only the great hand of Mother Nature will strike and shake the ground for all to hear.' My beggar placed me upon his shoulders, foraging a path through the white thorn. They bowed to him with every strike of his blackthorn stick, clearing a path of light as the glowworms rested upon his feet. Oh, such power beneath me, as if we were going into battle to save mankind from a world that knows nothing but contempt for my beggar.

We arrived in all our glory at the rose tree where he placed me down. 'All you need this night, Bubbles, is faith.' As I watched my beggar stood his ground with his blackthorn, its crown jumping up and down in the palm of his hand. My beggar was ready to lay down his life to defend his world. A cloud of darkness was beginning to cover the hill, releasing terrifying, stretching shadows. They flanked my beggar that night as they stalked in silence. The fiery night sky had arrived with the hounds of hell looking for their masters.

'Let us cross that line of no return.' With one roar from my beggar, the blackthorn stick across his chest, he lunged forward, trapping all within his grasp with such strength. It brought a tear to my eye. As the hounds grabbed my beggar and ripped his clothes from his back, he fell to his knees from an almighty blow to the head delivered by a world that's gone mad.

I looked to the hill of blackthorn – it's now or never – and closed my eyes for a few seconds, thought it felt an eternity. I felt a gentle breeze like an awakening upon my face. I looked to the hill of blackthorn as it roared with an almighty clap of thunder that shook the ground beneath us, freezing everyone in terror. My beggar rose from his despair and shouted, 'Bubbles, it's your hill of blackthorn. It's calling you. Fly, Bubbles!'

I lifted into the air like a swallow. I was gone, the wind beneath my sails, soaring through the narrow path with its hidden, twisted roots. They slunk down in wait to capture their guilty pleasure of all those who trample upon them, oh, those fading voices of pain were out of reach in this world of mine. Man's best friend kept the trail alive but was no match for the cliff's edge as they leapt forward into the air, frothing at the mouth, snarling inches from my face. But I felt no fear. Mother Nature had me in her hand and glided me around the cliff's edge.

The skull cracker waited to greet the hounds of hell with open arms, while I made it to the top of Blackthorn Hill. I took my rightful place upon this great slab of stone for all to see. 'Yes, I am Bubbles of Blackthorn Hill.' I placed such wilderness between my lips, freshness blooming on my tongue, and I let loose a shout for all to hear. 'I am free!' The heavens opened with white hail crashing down.

I drove the invading force from Blackthorn Hill back into the Valley of the White Horse, leaving nothing but blinding whiteness. I searched for my beggar There he was, covered in white and a splash of red. 'Oh, my beggar,' I said as I dropped to my knees and cradled his head in my arms. 'How could someone show such anger and hatred to my beggar?' I screamed with passion, shattering my bitterness into the white softness of snow.

My beggar opened his eyes and looked upon me, saying, 'I thought I lost you, Bubbles, forever, to a world that never knows what it's like to be free.' I tried to lift my beggar, but only came crashing down onto the snow and found myself stretched out. All I could do was look at the heavens and watch the snow drift towards its final resting place just like us.

I started to smile, I didn't know why, followed by a hearty laugh, thinking that maybe this was the end for me and my beggar. Maybe we never had a chance in this world. Oh, but what a picture of beauty to leave it with a smile on my face and nothing else. It was worth it; nothing else mattered to me. I had a great time, even if this was the end. Then, I spotted a little robin land a few feet from us, chirping loudly.

'Well, Mr. Robin, what seems to be the matter? If I were only gifted with the strength you have in your little wings, I would fly with my beggar and bring him home.' I watched him take flight and land on my biggest hat and start to dance with such delight. I had to sit up, leaning forward. 'Is there something you'd like to share with us, Mr. Robin, this night?' I felt a little slight movement underneath me as if I was beginning to slide a little. Looking behind me, I had crushed into the snow into a narrow path. Turning back my little robin, I said, 'Oh, Mr. Robin. You are a clever lad for giving us the gift of flight.'

Quickly, I grabbed my beggar, turning him in an upright position in front of me, stretching out his legs, and leant back. With a little shuffle, we started to slide along nice and steady. It was perfect. I admired the magic of the snow landing on the treetops, the mountains, and the valleys as a slight breeze nudged us along.

As we started to pick up speed, I looked over my beggar's shoulders; the hill had chosen the steepest path for us. The path dipped into the ground; there was no way out. As I held onto my beggar for dear life, flying swiftly downhill, I could feel the hair standing on my head as my beggar was covered in a cloud of white, blinding, powdery snow. All I could do was trust my hill of blackthorn and hope for the best. That we were going to have a perfect landing right in front of my beggar's door.

As we flew past the angry mob, their searing flames sizzling out as they fell into the bank of wet, slushy snow, I looked at the sky and spotted the line of smoke. We were nearly there; all I had to do was drop my feet into the snow. It had to be perfect timing. I raised my hands to the sky and closed my eyes. I had to believe in myself. 'It's now or never.' I plunged my feet down as if dropping an anchor. With an almighty crash of snow, we had stopped.

Opening my eyes, my beggar was missing. There wasn't a sign of him. 'Maybe I've lost him coming down the hill,' I fretted.

'Well, Bubbles, are you going to sit in the snow for the rest of the evening?' I twisted toward his voice. He was covered from head to toe in snow, shaking it from his beard, and reached out his hand to me and gave me the lift I needed. We had made it to my beggar's house.

'What of the angry mob?'

'Don't worry, Bubbles, we have all the time we need.'

We watched the snow pile high into drifts, blocking all paths to my beggar's world. Winter had arrived in all its glory, just in the nick of time. Dusting ourselves off and getting our colour back upon our cheeks, I looked at my beggar.

'How did you know the hill of blackthorn would save us tonight?'

'Well, Bubbles, one can't live without the other,' he said.

Something had changed for my beggar that night. I could see it in his eyes with my listening watch. He was not alone, even within the silence of winter. I hoped the arrival of the snowdrops would be a welcome break, their buds peeking out and bringing a joyful touch of spring.

'Oh,' the voices within him said, 'My beggar, remember us? Outstanding! You have risen to the occasion. You protected this world of ours with all your glory. You truly are the master of all, the beggar of Blackthorn Hill, the last of your kind. You've proven your loyalty to us once again. You've risen to the occasion with a sense of pride upon your shoulders, reaching out with your hands of strength to protect this world of ours. Yes, you will be rewarded with eternal love. But what of this child, now, beggar? Oh, such innocence at your side is nothing more than weakness. But fear not. Trust is within our hand. We can gift the child with great understanding and knowledge of our ways; he will have such loyalty to you. He will strike anything that stands before him, as so you for us. Why not? What do you always say – What's in it for you? Everything, my beggar. Whatever you desire without question, in exchange for such loyalty to us. Such loyalty will never be tested as long as you rise with us and fight for this world that we hold so dear to our hearts. And if not, we will take the child you call Bubbles. Right over that cliff edge; he will no longer be any concern to you.'

As I listen to their howling winds of terror, I pulled from my faith in Blackthorn Hill an innocence. One that would hopefully set alight like a new spark. One that would surely burn this world of theirs into nothing more than a pile of ash. And I would be the master of all and take back such a child that's rightfully mine.

A sense of sadness had gripped my beggar as if his mind was troubled. I could see it in his eyes as if he was searching for long past dreams that could have changed his life and set him free.

As my beggar gazed upon me, he said, 'Oh, Bubbles. I have been blinded in this world of mine, and now I see clearly because of the sparkle of your eyes upon me. You must leave this place and go to my brother's house. Set him free. He too is blinded by the bright lights. Just like me, he has forgotten what we really hold dear.'

All he could do in this world of was listen to those voices within as if they were demons holding him to ransom. I had lost my beggar to those voices. He was so gripped by the fear of losing a great treasure over a cliff edge that he would not speak of to me. Not even I had the strength to reach my beggar; he would never be free while I was by his side.

Yes, my time had come to leave my beggar of Blackthorn Hill. If only I could close my eyes and live my life in peace with my beggar in this perfect world. But, like my beggar said, I must go to the world that never sleeps under its blood-red sky, even though it will resent me with every twist and turn.

'Don't be afraid. My brother wears his heart upon his sleeve. I want to give you my greatest gift. It has brought us such joy and riches.' He handed me his beggar's bowl. 'Bring it to my brother's table of silver and gold. Feast from it every night. When the time is right, he will eat from such a wooden bowl will sing with joy, remembering his calling from Blackthorn Hill. And then we will reunite to live in peace in a world that will give us everything our hearts desire. Yes, it will be a new beginning for all of us.'

But I know my beggar's heart wasn't going to change. Dark forces were at hand and there was no time for me. I couldn't even catch his eye when I called to him. He looked away without a sound as if he had been frozen in time. Just a flicker of his hand as he searched the ground frantically. I wondered what could be more important to my beggar than me. He dropped to his knees, saying, 'I got them, Bubbles,' and slipped an old pair of shoes upon my bare feet.

'Remember, Bubbles, when lost, take them off and lay your feet upon the ground. You will always gain the strength to find the right path and walk among the gentle giants, sharing wisdom and knowledge will everyone. In return for such delight, they will provide shade from a blistering sun. Yes, there are the mothers of falling stars that I have collected who now stand together as one in this great wood of mine. Lay your hand upon them. They will speak to you and show you the way with their strong branches that reach for the sky. They will give you all the knowledge you need in this new world. Stand under them and climb to their highest branches with a sense of pride for who you are. Gaze upon their rooftops and think of me, calling you home. And you will smile and say, "Not even my beggar's brother's apple can fall too far from Blackthorn Hill. Even in the flames of hell,"' he said, smiling at me. 'Never mind; it will be grand. Think of the mouse in the bottle; what might seem to be an eternity to them is no time at all.'

I raised my hand over my beggar's head without touching him as if trying to capture his spirit and set it free like the robin with his wings. I would never be alone, not even in the darkest of times in this new world. My time had come to leave my beggar's house. All I had to do was cross that great bridge of tears, never forgetting those wise words my beggar said to me the first time we climbed Blackthorn Hill together. 'Never look behind you, Bubbles. The past might steal your dreams for a new beginning.' But my beggar couldn't hide his expression from me as I captured his shadow, stepping into it as if we were one. 'I will return and set you free,' I thought as the doors swung open to this new world, my heart heavy. I hoped I would have the inner strength to take the almighty first step. As this stranger's eyes were firmly fixed upon my beggar and challenged me, 'What is he to you?'

'He's everything.'

The End

About the Author

Hello, they all call me Tiger Man. I'm married with three children and a very patient wife. I started writing this book during lockdown in 2020, which was a great help and kept me away from the paint brush! Being left-handed, you know how it is, as sometimes I feel I live in a world that was only made for the right-handed. I hope you like the book, and may it remind us all of the beggar's great tree of knowledge, as our silence can sometimes be our strength, no matter what.

Taidhg McCarthy.

www.ingramcontent.com/pod-product-compliance
Ingram Content Group UK Ltd.
Pitfield, Milton Keynes, MK11 3LW, UK
UKHW042021211224
452733UK00001B/92